LYLE NICHOLSON

SUSPECTS
AND
LIARS

VINCI
BOOKS

By Lyle Nicholson

Bernadette Callahan Series

Vinci Books

vinci-books.com

Published by Vinci Books Ltd in 2025

1

A CIP catalogue record for this book is available from the British Library.
Paperback ISBN: 9781036707811

Chapter One

Red Deer, Alberta, Canada

July, 2 years ago

Eric Chan fell from the balcony of his tenth-floor apartment at a speed of 65 mph. His trip of one hundred feet to the ground took just 2.95 seconds. A woman with a baby missed being the landing point for Eric's body because she pushed her stroller away from a man smoking a cigarette on a bench.

Eric hit with a thump on the pavement that jolted the bystanders out of the peace of their quiet evening and had them dialing 911. There was nothing anyone could do for him.

There was no bounce, no groan, no whoosh of air expelled from his lungs. The coroner's report would find he'd ingested enough barbiturates to put an elephant to sleep.

How Eric had climbed over the edge of the balcony of his tenth-floor apartment was a mystery. However, it was determined that since there was no forced entry or CCTV of visitors, Eric must have mustered a Herculean effort to kill himself. An email he left behind claimed he was sorry, but gambling had taken over his life.

The coroner placed a simple line of 'death by suicide' on the report. He had quietly mentioned to the police in attendance, "it was not the fall that killed him, but the sudden stop."

Eric Chan's case would remain listed as a suicide, given a number, registered with the Canadian Bureau of Statistics, and left for his parents to grieve their loss.

No one thought to open the case until Detective Bernadette Callahan returned to active duty two years later, on a frosty morning in November. Her child was now two years old. She'd been happy as a mother, living on a farm with her loving husband Chris, and three horses, a dog and a barn cat, but Eric's death bothered her.

Eric had worked for Armand Paradis Transport when Detective Callahan investigated the company for human trafficking. That investigation had gone cold. Today, Detective Bernadette Callahan of the Royal Canadian Mounted Police Department was about to add some heat.

Chapter Two

Present day, Red Deer, Alberta, mid-November.

Bernadette Callahan sighed as she rolled out of bed. Chris was already up, getting breakfast ready and playing with Raven, their two-year-old daughter. Sounds of Raven's laughter mingled with the clang of pots and pans.

The little girl was developing fast and was considered gifted by her pediatrician. She'd taken to mirroring her dad's movements in the kitchen and following her mother around their small ten-acre farm to tend to the horses. Bernadette made her way to the master bathroom, pulled off her nightgown and turned on the shower.

She examined herself in the mirror. A recent tattoo of a raven had covered the scar from the gunshot wound to her abdomen. Bernadette rubbed her tummy and felt soreness in the area around the design of a beautiful black raven with its wings spread. The idea for the tattoo came to her the day she decided to return to work with the Serious Crimes Division of the Royal Canadian Mounted Police.

They took on the most serious crimes in the little town of Red Deer, Alberta, with a population of over one hundred thousand, on the Canadian prairies with the Red Deer River snaking through it that originated from the Rocky Mountains in Banff National Park.

Summers were hot, and winters were cold. Bernadette and Chris had finished the renovations on their farmhouse, which they had named Blue Sky Acres, put in a large garden, built a chicken coop to house twenty chickens that kept growing and saw the birth of a foal that was now two years old and galloping over the fields.

Their daughter Raven had grown into the little farm as if it was a magical wonderland. She helped to feed the chickens, harvest eggs, pluck weeds (that were often seedlings) and brush as much of the horses as she could reach. It was only the top of the horse's legs, but they didn't mind.

Sprocket, the big German Shepherd and Pepper, the barn cat, often accompanied Raven between the barn, the coop, and the house. Harvey Mawer and his partner, Ava Dubois, their neighbors, owned the old carriage house in the back. Although Raven thought she was on her own, Harvey and Ava were always watching her or following from behind.

Bernadette was both anxious and excited. She was going back to work solving crimes and protecting Canada's citizens from general mayhem. But to do so, she had to leave this little piece of idyllic paradise with her family.

Her sigh this morning was leaving her only child for the day. They hadn't been apart since her birth. Raven had been a miracle. Callahan had given birth to her after being shot in the abdomen by a suspect. The bullet had missed

Raven and lodged in Callahan's liver. She recovered, and Raven was born two weeks early.

They'd been through a lot together, and now Bernadette would leave to pursue the same suspect that had shot her. Only her partner knew what her motives were. She pulled on her jeans and shirt and strapped on her bullet-proof vest. Today, she'd pick up her gun and badge.

She looked at herself in the mirror and smiled. "This mommy is going to kick some ass!"

Chris was slicing oranges, and Raven was playing with Sprocket when Bernadette entered the kitchen. She hugged and kissed Raven and ruffled Sprocket's ears.

"You look in fighting form," Chris said as he placed the oranges on a tray with strawberries and swiveled to grab the toast that had popped up from the toaster.

Bernadette poured herself some coffee, added two sugars with cream, and took a sip. "Yes, after two years of changing diapers, chasing Raven round the farm and nursing sick chickens, I am ready to enter the adult world of daily crime."

"So, how do you feel?" Chris asked.

Bernadette sidled up beside him and whispered, "I'm terrified. The moment I walk out the door without Raven, I think my heart might break. We've been inseparable for two years. How do I handle this?"

Chris put his big arm around her. He was over six feet, with a weightlifter's physique, curly dark hair, and hazel brown eyes from his Greek parents. "Enjoy your day. Try not to rough up too many bad guys."

"You are so funny. But seriously, how have you coped?"

Chris kissed her on the forehead. "I go to my work as a forest ranger in the Rocky Mountain Reserve, knowing I'm coming back to the most beautiful girls in the world."

"Okay, now you're going to make it harder to get out the door."

"Look, we've talked about this for weeks. Harvey and Ava have offered to take care of Raven during the day. She calls them uncle and auntie like they are family."

"If we didn't need the money, I'd never leave this place," Bernadette said

"Is this the same woman I met who never wanted to marry or settle down?"

Bernadette munched toast and sipped her coffee. "Yeah, my mother's instincts kicked in with our little girl. Who saw that coming?"

"Well, I like the transition but take it easy today. You don't have to take down every criminal your first day on the job," Chris said.

"Sure, I promise." She sat with Raven for a while, brushed her shiny dark hair and wiped the food off her face. The little girl had the dark complexion of Bernadette from her Native Cree ancestry and green eyes from Bernadette's Irish father. But the dark curly hair was from her father's Greek side. She seemed more beautiful every day and harder to be away from.

Bernadette hugged and kissed Raven goodbye and felt like her heart was being ripped out. Then, she put on her coat and boots and headed out the door. Once she fired up her Jeep, she placed a call to her partner, Evanston.

"What have you got?" Bernadette said when Evanston answered.

"It's just like you figured it. Eric Chan's parents claim he never gambled a day in his life. No one caught that in the report two years ago."

"Did anyone ask the question?"

"We conducted the interview over the phone. Our interpreter is Cantonese, and they speak Mandarin. There was a loss in translation."

"Great, I'll take this to Chief Durham when I get in," Bernadette said.

"No worries. I dropped the file on his desk last night. Durham said he'd hand the case over to us, but he wants to know who we are going after for suspects."

"They murdered Chan because he knew something about Armand Paradis's involvement with human trafficking. We both know that."

"You're going to push a lot of buttons your first day back at the job."

"Yeah, did you miss me?"

"It's been too quiet here. Just shooting and stabbings. You'll be a breath of fresh air if you try to nab a big fish."

"Great, I'll see you soon," Bernadette said. She pulled the Jeep out of the garage and headed down the highway onto the road into town. A smile spread over her face. "Momma is on the hunt."

Chapter Three

Large snowflakes splatted on the windshield in the early morning darkness as Bernadette drove to work at the main RCMP Detachment in Red Deer. Her shift would be from 8 a.m. to 5 p.m., as the Serious Crime Division chose their own schedule. But to her, the shift ended when she had closure on a suspect or brought in fresh evidence.

Today would be a test of her commitment to the job and her daughter and husband. There was a gnawing sensation in her gut as the sun threw a red glow over the horizon. Did she have the mettle to do her job and be a good mother? She was about to find out.

She parked her Jeep in the police parking lot and walked into the Serious Crime unit. Evanston, her long-time partner, sat hunched over reports, coffee in hand, wearing a frown. She had two teenage boys and a loving husband who worked for the post office. He made sure the boys got to their football and hockey practices when she had to stay at work.

Bernadette poured herself a coffee and joined her.

"Hey Evanston, why the frown? You look like your hockey team lost the final."

Evanston looked up from her file. "Hey, Bernie, I didn't see you come in, you know I always have a sour face when reading case files. So, how's your little girl?"

"She's fine. It was hard to leave her this morning. I hope this gets easier."

"It never does. I've felt like I put my heart in a box every morning that I had to leave my two boys over the years. But it's part of the job. You'll find it gets better with time."

"Thanks for the pep talk. When can we meet Chief Durham?"

Evanston laughed. "Yes, I see you want to get down to business. The chief is in his office. Where do you want to start on the case."

"Right back at the beginning. I'm calling Paradis Transport when they open at 9 a.m. and setting up interviews with everyone who worked with Chan."

Evanston pushed the file on her desk to Bernadette. "This file is from two years ago. There were a lot of *faulty memories and people who claimed they were not involved with Chan.*"

Bernadette opened the file and looked over the names. "I wonder if Kaitlin Godwin is still the head of Human Resources there. She was the one who introduced me to Eric Chan."

Evanston punched keys on her computer. "Paradis Transport lists her as their head of H.R. if their website is up to date. It's a good starting point."

Bernadette leaned back in her chair and sipped her coffee. "My God, it feels good to be back on the hunt. I missed this so much."

Evanston chuckled. "See how easy it is to transition

between mother and hard-driving investigator? You're going to be back in the saddle in no time!"

Bernadette smiled, refreshed her coffee, and spent a few minutes greeting the investigators in her division before heading into Chief of Detectives Sergeant Jerry Durham's office.

Durham was mid-fifties with a son and daughter in university. His wife was an administrator at Red Deer Polytechnic, and they'd worked hard to put their kids into excellent schools. Jerry was adamant his kids didn't pursue a life in law enforcement. He figured one family member, meaning him, was enough of a sacrifice. He hoped they'd pursue careers in banking or accounting and come home at night without seeing the carnage of humanity every day.

Durham had gone bald. He'd given himself over to a buzzed head shave every day and couldn't help running his hand over the back of his smooth head as he talked or listened. It was a nervous tick that Bernadette found strange.

He looked up from his desk as she entered. "You ready for the real world again?"

Bernadette's' lips went into a tight line. "Yeah, no one is ever ready for the world of police work. I'm sure I'll adjust back to it in time."

Durham sat back in his chair and leveled his gaze at Bernadette. "I'm aware of how badly you want to investigate the death of Eric Chan."

"You understand it involves more than just Eric Chan."

Durham ran his hand over the back of his head. "You won't let the Paradis brothers murders alone, will you?"

"I started their file two years ago, and the brass shut me down. I'm going in hard on Chan's death—I know it was murder. There's a link somewhere in the Paradis Transport Company. I'm going to dig."

Durham let his eyes rest on the desk for a moment to collect his thoughts. "You've been one of my best investigators, and I trust your instincts. But please don't piss off half the city interviewing suspects."

"The only people I interview who get upset with my methods are the ones who are lying to me," Bernadette said with a smile.

Durham's large hand traveled from the back of his head to rest on his forehead. His eyes closed for a second, then opened. "Okay, I look forward to your reports. And thanks for returning to the force. We've been losing members in droves to early retirement. I have just enough personnel to cover our shifts. You're a great help."

"You're welcome, Chief. Now, I'll be on my way. I've got some interviews to do," Bernadette said.

By 10 a.m., she was heading down the Queen Elizabeth Highway toward the Industrial district. She'd called ahead to book an appointment with Kaitlin Godwin, the head of Human Resources. Two years ago, she felt a suspicion about Godwin. Today, there'd be serious questions about the death of Eric Chan.

Bernadette rolled up to the head office of Paradis Transport and surveyed the parking lot. The parking stall of Armand Paradis was empty. He was on her list to interview, but he'd take more effort. Two years ago, he'd threatened her with his lawyer. That was fine with her. It meant Paradis would pay a lawyer over five hundred dollars an hour to sit outside a room as she dragged out an interview with him on hard chairs and terrible coffee. She looked forward to the meeting.

The receptionist took Bernadette to Kaitlin Godwin's office. Kaitlin stood up and greeted her with a handshake that felt clammy and shaky. The woman was noticeably pregnant.

"I see our situations are different," Bernadette said. "When I was here several years ago, I was the one that was pregnant. When are you due?"

Kaitlin rubbed her tummy and smiled. "Not until March, but my partner and I are excited."

"I'm sure you are. You look amazing, of course. Now, you probably know I'm here to follow up on the death of Eric Chan," Bernadette said as she pulled out her notepad.

"Yes, of course. That was terrible. His parents and everyone in our office were, naturally, devastated. None of us imagined he could do that."

"Are you speaking of the alleged suicide?"

"Well, yes. Of course. What else could it have been?"

Bernadette paused and waited. She held Kaitlin's gaze and let the silence grow. It would become deafening soon. No one liked silence.

"How about murder?" Bernadette asked.

"Murder! How is that possible?" Kaitlin blurted.

"Let me state some facts we discovered. The number of drugs in Eric's body would have made it impossible for him to climb over his balcony."

"But it was determined a suicide."

"I've returned to duty, and I've opened the case as a murder investigation. You can expect me to ask for every file in this company that Eric Chan was involved with. I'm sure your company lawyers will jump all over this. But don't worry; I have our crown prosecutors drafting up a search warrant that will have this company crawling with police to pull your files."

"But that will shut us down. Mr. Paradis will be furious."

"Yes, I'm sure he will, but there's no avoiding it. Tell me about Eric Chan."

"He came to me with an invoice for a shipping container that was being refitted; he found it strange."

"Why is that?"

"The container was being refitted to transport humans."

Chapter Four

Kaitlin got up and closed her door, then sat back down and lowered her voice. "I always figured there was something suspicious about Eric's death."

"Why is that?"

"A subsidiary of our company owned the apartment that Eric rented. Look, I don't know how much I can tell you. If someone could get to Eric, they could get to me as well. Everyone in this company was terrified when we heard about his death."

"Who are you afraid of?"

"You know who it is. You asked me about her when you entered this office several years back. It's what got you in trouble."

"You mean Hanna Winter, the woman from Berlin? You think she was behind the murder of Eric Chan?"

Kaitlin pulled a tissue out of a box and blew her nose. Her hand was shaking. "You do not know how many people in this office feared Hanna when she worked here seven years ago. We knew she was close with Armand. He was infatuated with her; she was thirty years younger and beautiful, and she appeared to have control over him.

"You could have mentioned this to the police years ago. Maybe you could have saved Chan," Bernadette said.

Kaitlin sniffed and dabbed her eyes. "His death will haunt me forever. But don't you see? We know there's no way you can prove it."

"Help me get to Hanna Winter. Give me enough to dig up the evidence of her hand in Chan's murder."

"I doubt I have anything for you, but Sanjay Chadha was the head of accounting. Before Chan's death, he accused him of billing Paradis Transport with over two hundred thousand in fake invoices. Chadha discovered that the money was being directed to Chan's bank account."

"Do you remember what Chan said about the accusations?"

"He came into my office—he claimed the charges were false. He was furious and scared," Kaitlin said.

"Was he afraid of being fired?"

"Of course, but it was more than that. He said he thought he'd seen someone who looked like Hanna Winter with Armand late one night in the parking lot. Soon after that, he claimed he was seeing strange invoices come through for refitted shipping containers."

"Who did he talk to about his findings?"

"He said he went to Armand Paradis and asked him what this new container was for. Armand laughed and said it was a new transport idea he'd come up with."

"Did Chan let it go?"

"No, three more invoices came through for the same thing. Chan went to Sanjay about them. He told me Sanjay looked nervous and told him this was none of his concern."

"Where is Sanjay Chadha now?"

"He left two weeks ago."

"Did he give his notice?"

Kaitlin shook her head. "No, he shot out of here fast. One day he was here, the next day, he emailed saying he had to return to India to get married. I think he was having one of those arranged marriages they have over there."

"Will you testify to the conversations you have had with Chan?"

Kaitlin shook her head. "If I do, my testimony will be hearsay. The only one who can give you anything will be Sanjay. He's the only one who saw the invoices, and he'll know who set up Chan. I hire, promote, and fire people. My word against the mighty Armand Paradis and cute little Hanna Winter means nothing. And I have an unborn child to protect."

"Do you know where I can locate Sanjay?"

Kaitlin clicked the keys on her computer. "He has an aunt in Edmonton. I can give you, her address; he put her in as his contacts. He might still be in Canada. If he's gone to India, I doubt he'll ever come back."

Bernadette wrote the information for Sanjay and looked up at Katlin. "If I can get Sanjay to corroborate your story, would you make a statement regarding your conversation with Chan?"

"If Sanjay Chadha knows where the invoices for the containers are, he'll know how Chan was framed—sure, I'll make a full statement. I've had many sleepless nights over Chan's death. I'd love to find out who caused his death. My bets are on Hanna Winter."

She got in her unmarked Jeep and called the number of

Sanjay Chadha. A woman answered, "Hello, Chadha residence."

"Hello, may I speak to Sanjay Chadha, please?" Bernadette asked. Her mind was racing to come up with a plan to get Sanjay's aunt to speak to him.

"Sanjay is not here; he has gone to the airport."

"Oh yes, I heard he was leaving for his wedding. I want to give him a gift. Do you think I could make it in time? My gift is quite large." Bernadette cringed at her lie, but she wanted Chadha.

"Of course, he is on the 5:25 p.m. KLM flight to Amritsar, India. Should I contact him and tell him to wait for you?"

"Oh no, the office put a cash gift of five thousand and one dollar together and sent it to me to give to him. We want it to be a surprise," Bernadette said. She remembered that a gift of cash at an Indian wedding must have a one dollar at the end, which means the money will grow.

"But are you not in Red Deer? How will you come, he must board his plane at 4:30 p.m.,"

the woman said.

"Not to worry, I live just on the outskirts of Edmonton. The office forwarded the money to me to bring to him. I hope you won't ruin our surprise."

"Your secret is very safe with me. Thank you."

"No, thank you," Bernadette said. She ended the call and called Durham. "I found a prime suspect. We've got four hours to get a warrant and stop him from getting on a plane to India from the Edmonton Airport."

"Text me his information and the reason for the warrant. So glad you're back; things were getting boring."

Chapter Five

Bernadette pushed the unmarked police jeep to the max on the Queen Elizabeth II highway with the lights and siren on. Traffic moved over to let them pass. Evanston was in the passenger's seat with her cell phone.

Her phone rang. She answered and listened, then put the phone on her lap. "The judge won't give us a warrant. He said we have only hearsay evidence," Evanston said.

"Damn, is that the judge that plays golf with Armand Paradis?"

"Could be, but you don't want to say that to anyone else but me."

"Okay, we play the hard way—we use 'reasonable grounds to detain,'" Bernadette said.

"He'll be out inside of twenty-four hours," Evanston said.

"Yeah, but I get to sweat him," Bernadette said.

"Call airport security and tell them we have a suspect to interview in a murder case."

Evanston made a call, talked for a few minutes, then raised her eyes. "I got in touch with Edmonton Airport Security. They checked the passenger list, and Sanjay was there. He's in business class and getting ready to get on the plane."

"Do you think they could hold the plane for us?" Bernadette asked.

"They're asking if we have a warrant."

"Put them on speakerphone," Bernadette said.

"This is Corporal Bunsen of the Canadian Airport Transport Security; how may I help you?"

"Hi, corporal, this is Detective Callahan with Red Deer Serious Crimes Division. We are in pursuit of a person who we believe can help us solve a murder case with links to human trafficking. We have no warrant, but Sanjay Chadha is our only lead. Can you hold that plane?"

"If you don't have a warrant, I can't hold the plane. My C.O. goes ape-shit when we don't have proper cause—"

"You want cause, Corporal Bunsen? A person connected to Chadha put a bullet in me two years ago and almost killed my unborn child—how's that for the cause?"

"I'll see what I can do," Bunsen said. A minute later, he came back on the phone. "I got you twenty minutes. My tarmac security team will report debris near the plane. You better haul ass to get here; that's the best I can do."

"Copy that. On our way," Bernadette said. She pressed her foot on the accelerator. The Jeep hit 180 KM.

Evanston shook her head. "First day, and already you got a lead in the case. Just remember, we have families to go home to."

"No worries, the airport exit is ahead; I'm slowing down." Bernadette slowed enough to take the exit ramp without the Jeep wheels squealing. Evanston held onto the door handle as the vehicle's tires bit into the pavement to stay upright.

The Jeep roared up to the departure level. They got out and ran for the International Departures. Bernadette flashed her badge at security and ran down the concourse toward the KLM flight.

Evanston lagged her, muttering, "Why the hell do they have to put these damn flights so far away?"

Bernadette ran into the departures area and flagged the security officer to identify herself.

"Your guy just got on the plane. He's sitting in seat 2D," Officer Bunsen said.

Bernadette flashed her badge to the flight attendants and to the captain. "We won't keep you long."

She walked into the large compartment of business class. Passengers were settling into their spacious seats that were encompassed in a pod, drinking champagne. They stared at Bernadette as if she had intruded.

She ignored them and walked to seat 2D. "Sanjay Chadha, I am detaining you on suspicion you were involved in a crime to commit fraud at Paradis Transport. I'm taking you into custody of the Red Deer Serious Crimes Division of the RCMP."

"But you cannot do this. What charges do you have? You cannot take me off this plane. I'm flying to my wedding in India," Chadha protested.

"Sorry, but you'll have to tell your bride she'll have to wait. You and I are going to have some serious discussions."

Chadha set his glass of champagne down, set his Bose

headset in the pod's console and took his aluminum Tumi carry-on bag out of the overhead. Everything about him looked aggravated to Bernadette, which could mean was he guilty or pissed he was being pulled from his flight.

Chapter Six

They rode back to Red Deer in silence. Chadha was in the back of the vehicle. He had settled down in the past hour after shouting and protesting the first thirty minutes of the drive.

Evanston broke the silence. "You going to call Chris?"

Bernadette looked down at the time on the vehicle's dashboard. It was now six thirty. She'd promised to be home by five.

"Damn, I told myself I'd text him and Raven after we took Chadha into custody," Bernadette said, shaking her head. "On my first day back at work, I'm struggling with balancing my responsibilities as a mother."

"Don't worry, it will get worse. Want to pull over and call Chris by the road? Maybe take some time to tell him what you're doing?"

"We're almost in Red Deer. I'll call him after we process Chadha."

"What do you mean by process me?" Chadha said from the back seat.

"I wish to contact my lawyer. You have my phone—this is illegal. I am a Canadian citizen with rights. I demand my phone and to meet with my lawyer. You all will sweep the streets tomorrow morning."

"You'll get your call once we are at RCMP headquarters, Mr. Chadha," Evanston said. "We have confiscated your phone as possible evidence and thank you for letting us know alternative occupations are waiting for us."

They rolled into the RCMP garage and Bernadette took Chadha into processing, then put him in an interview room. Once he was squared away, she went to meet with Durham.

"Do you think you'll get something out of him?" Durham asked.

"I'm not sure. He's pretty upset over missing his flight, but there's something about him I'm not sure about."

"What's that?" Durham asked.

"I wonder how it's possible for a guy like Chadha, who was a top accountant at Paradis Transport, pulling in maybe one hundred grand a year to be taking a business class trip to India. That costs over ten grand. He also had an expensive carry-on bag that cost over a thousand dollars. He is spending way more than he can afford or has an undisclosed source of money."

"You have less than twenty-four hours to find out," Durham said.

"Yeah, I'm going to need a lot of coffee, damn, I need to make a phone call," Bernadette said. A wave of guilt crashed over her as she remembered she still hadn't called home. The rush of apprehending Chadha and the interview had blurred the lines of her focus.

She took out her phone, inhaled deeply, and called home. Chris answered on the first ring, "Hey, what's happening?"

Bernadette found a quiet corner in the hallway near the interview rooms. "So sorry. We had a break in the Chan murder. Evanston and I have a person of interest to interview, and I'm going to be a while."

"I'm fine with it. But Raven has been asking for you since five. Can you talk to her?" Chris said.

Bernadette closed her eyes, her hand tightened around the phone.

"Hi, Mommy," Raven said. "When are you coming home?"

Bernadette held back tears. "My work is taking longer than I expected. I'll come home as soon as I can, but it might take some time."

"Okay, Mommy, I'll send my Raven to protect you."

"A raven, but isn't that your special one?" Bernadette asked. She'd shared the story of how a raven had protected her in a vehicle accident two years ago. Bernadette told her that Ravens were special to the Cree Natives and would protect her. The little girl had developed an imaginary raven for herself after Bernadette had one tattooed on her stomach.

"Yes, but I'm sending him to you. I'm safe with Daddy, so you can have him for the night. Don't forget to bring him home."

"I won't, my little angel. I'll see you as soon as I can."

Evanston walked by as Bernadette ended her call and collapsed against the wall.

"Looks like you called home. How'd it go?"

"Like a punch to the gut," Bernadette replied in a whisper.

Evanston nodded her head. "Never gets easier. Let's go interview our suspect."

Chapter Seven

Bernadette Callahan walked into the small interview room by herself. Sanjay Chadha sat at a white metal table. It was clear from the constant fidgeting of his fingers that he was nervous. He was mid-thirties, had a slight build, and a modern-styled haircut.

"I don't get why I can't have a lawyer here during this interview," Sanjay said.

Bernadette placed a pad and pen on the table and stared at him for a moment to let him settle down. "Because the Canadian legal system only requires a lawyer to accompany a minor. You are well over eighteen, Mr. Chadha. Now, can we begin, or do you wish to voice more complaints? I have all night."

"No, let's proceed. My lawyer told me you would try to trick me into confessing things. I want to express my extreme displeasure regarding this procedure," Sanjay said.

"Of course, duly noted," Bernadette said as she scribbled an illegible note on her pad.

Sanjay leaned forward and couldn't make out what she had written. He sighed and sunk back into his chair.

Bernadette activated the recording and introduced herself, her rank, and the others present before starting.

"Mr. Chadha, how long have you been an accountant for Paradis Trucking?"

"Why don't you get straight to the point? This is not a job interview," Sanjay said with disdain in his voice. "If we wrap this up tonight, I'll be there for the start of the wedding ceremonies. Indian weddings run for over three days."

Bernadette opened a file with a sheaf of papers she'd taken from another detective's desk. She placed her hands over the files so Sanjay couldn't see them.

"We believe you were involved in a plan to frame Mr. Eric Chan with embezzled funds from Paradis Transport. Information has come to our division that Chan discovered strange shipping containers for human beings. Soon after, someone transferred money into his account from bogus invoices, leading to his termination."

She looked hard at Sanjay. "How am I doing with the facts? Do you want me to get to the part where a witness claims Chan's blood is on your hands?"

"You are just fishing," Sanjay said. "My lawyer told me if you had anything, you would have arrested me with a proper warrant."

"I know your lawyer, Felicity Haynsworth. She likely informed you that if you wait in our jail cell, she'll arrange for your release in the morning."

Sanjay sat back in his chair and smiled.

"You haven't answered me, Mr. Chadha. If you think we have nothing, please press your luck. I'm sending this file to Canadian Security and Intelligence Services. They love to investigate things like shipping containers meant to transport humans. Did you work for Paradis Transport two years ago when we busted a ring of human traffickers in Calgary? Armand Paradis's hands were clean that time, but I'll bet we can find some juicy stuff in your accounting files."

Chadha sat in silence. He stared at his hands and massaged his fingers.

Bernadette leaned forward. "Why did you leave the company suddenly? Was it because I reopened the case?"

Chadha's head rocketed up. He stared at Bernadette. "Armand Paradis, my boss, thinks you are the devil and out to get him."

"Do you think you'll get caught in something illegal? You know, if you make a deal with us, we can provide immunity," Bernadette suggested.

"I don't know what you mean. I don't know what you are accusing me of."

Bernadette stared at Chadha. "The judge has the power to dismiss false accusations in court. Look me in the eye, Sanjay. Tell me I'm lying."

Chadha put his hands to his face and shook his head. "What will you do to me?"

"If you get implicated in human trafficking, you will face many years of imprisonment."

Sanjay sighed and slouched in his chair. "Had I not spent so much time dealing with unresolved matters, I would be in India, and all of this would feel like a nightmare."

"Would you like to address the events involving Chan and your decision to leave the company?" Bernadette asked.

Chapter Eight

Chadha sipped water from a paper cup and leaned forward to look directly at Bernadette. "Eric Chan was my friend. We played hockey together and hung out at each other's places."

"So, what happened?"

"He found several strange invoices from Europe for refitting shipping containers with airplane-style chairs, water systems, toilets, and air handling. He couldn't figure it out. I realized that someone sent it to him in error because he's only a transport manager."

"To whose department should they have been sent?" Bernadette said.

"Well, that's what's crazy about the invoices. Nobody knew what it was about. Armand Paradis claimed it was only a model the company was working on, like a beta prototype. He said not to worry about it."

"But Chan dug into it. Is that what happened?" Bernadette said.

"Chan found active transport documents of the special

containers from the port of Hamburg to the port of Montreal. I must hand it to him; he was skilled at searching through records. I'm confident the CSIS will find everything. He presented me with evidence the containers had been shipped several times."

"Were you aware the containers transported humans?" Bernadette asked.

Chadha shook his head. "No one knows, but when Paradis discovered Chan and I had been in the files, he became extremely agitated. I've never seen him so mad."

"What did he say to you?"

"That the containers were none of our business. He was dealing in the transport of special items, and we needed to keep out of it."

"Why was Chan targeted? What did he do to aggravate Paradis?"

"Chan had many contacts in the overseas transport business. Once he reached out to them, he discovered the companies had been shipping the retrofitted containers for Paradis Transport. He gave me a list one night when we met for a beer after a hockey game."

"Why didn't he bring this to the police?"

"Chan was loyal to Paradis and couldn't believe his actions. He thought it had something to do with a previous employee. I don't remember her name."

"Hanna Winter? Was that the name?"

"Yes, I wasn't employed when she worked for the company, but there were rumors that Armand and she took part in illegal activities involving the transportation of immigrants from the International airport."

"You mean human trafficking?" Bernadette asked.

Sanjay's face became blank. "I thought Armand might

bring in illegal immigrants to help them out because he cared about them. I never thought he'd be involved."

"Involved in trafficking humans for profit. Is that what you wanted to say?"

Sanjay lowered his head. "What can you do for me if I testify?"

"We will offer you immunity from prosecution if your testimony does not implicate you in the death of Eric Chan. Does that satisfy you?"

"I did not kill Eric Chan," Sanjay said. "No one knows how it happened, but we have suspicions that Paradis hired someone from Romania. He's traveled to Bucharest many times in the past several years. And I've seen several strange-looking men here late at night in his office. And you must understand that Paradis is the proprietor of the apartment tower from which Chan fell."

"That is interesting information. You think someone turned off the CCTV camera in the building?" Bernadette asked.

Chadha shrugged. "That would not surprise me."

"Who produced the fake invoices and bank transactions to frame Chan?" Bernadette asked.

"It wasn't me. When someone brought the invoices and bank transactions to my attention, I was shocked."

"Who informed you?"

"Kaitlin Godwin. She told me we had a problem with Eric and that Armand Paradis was furious. He wanted him fired."

Bernadette leaned back. "I spoke with Kaitlin this morning."

"Ah, and she told you Eric was her friend, and she was trying to protect him. There is much you need to know about her."

Chapter Nine

"Kaitlin Godwin was the one who framed Eric Chan with the fake invoices for containers and the fraudulent bank transfers," Sanjay said.

"She stated it was you."

"No, she wants you to think it was me. She assumed I'd left the country, and I wouldn't tell you she was behind everything."

"Why would she do that?"

"She will do anything to protect Armand Paradis."

"She's a very loyal employee. What else is new?"

"You do not know the extent of her involvement."

"Try me. Tell me what she did."

Chadha rubbed his hands and looked at Bernadette. "First, her supposed partner is a sham. He is my lover."

Bernadette put her hand to her head. "Ah, just when I thought it couldn't get more confusing. So, you're not really heading to India to get married?"

Chadha looked at his fingers and rubbed a cuticle. "Well, yes, that much is true. But the wedding is a fake. My father suspects I am gay and threatened he'd cut me out of my inheritance if I refused. My intended bride prefers women, and I am a good cover for her. And this somehow, in the spirit of Indian culture makes two families happy."

"And why is Godwin living with your ex-lover?"

"He's not my ex; he is my lover. Kaitlin threatened to expose me to my family. She demanded my partner live with her to hide the fact that she was having an affair with a married man. She said once I was married in India, my lover could join me in six months."

Bernadette shook her head to clear her thoughts. "What does any of this have to do with Chan's death and containers built for human trafficking?"

"I'm giving you the facts. Kaitlin Godwin is the real mastermind behind the scheme to frame Chan."

"And why would she do that?"

"Because she is carrying the child of Armand Paradis," Chadha said.

Bernadette sat back in her chair. "Are you willing to testify that she carried out a plan to discredit Eric Chan and have him fired?"

"Yes, and I know how she had him killed," Chadha said.

"I'm listening."

"The night Eric Chan fell to his death I saw her with a package with his name on it. She told me she was taking it to his apartment."

"How will we find evidence she entered his apartment? Chan had locked the door."

"She had an apartment with Armand in that same building. There are no cameras in the hallways or the elevators, and the ones in the parking garage were disabled. Kaitlin's apartment was one floor below Chan's."

"How do you know this?"

"I used it to meet with my lover," Chadha said with a smile.

Bernadette looked at him. "I'm not sure if I'm writing a crime report or something out of a romance novel. Why did you withhold this information from the police?"

"Kaitlin threatened to expose me to my entire community. It would harm my family's reputation if they found out, and my chosen wife is quite wealthy. Her father paid for my business class ticket to India and expensive luggage," Chadha said. He glanced at the ceiling, then at Bernadette. "None of it matters now. All the truth will come out. But at least you will have the person responsible for the death of Eric Chan."

Bernadette pushed a pad of paper and pen toward Chadha. "I want you to write your statement regarding Kaitlin Godwin and leave nothing out." She got up and left the room.

Evanston was outside. "I listened from the other room; those are some convoluted entanglements."

"Yeah, who needs to binge on Netflix when you've got this kind of stuff going on? I'm going to write up my report. Can we send a uniform to pick up Kaitlin Godwin?"

Bernadette sat down with a coffee to type out her report on her computer. She tried to avoid looking at her watch, as it was three hours past her shift. The office was quiet as she wrote out the strange conversation with Sanjay Chadha and wondered what Kaitlin Godwin would offer. The night would be long.

Evanston came into the office. "We got a problem—Kaitlin Godwin is gone."

Chapter Ten

The stars were twinkling as Bernadette drove into Blue Sky Acres. Lights illuminated the house, yard, and barn, casting a warm glow on the snow. She parked the Jeep in the garage and let her feet take her to the barn for some horse therapy.

She didn't feel ready to face Chris and Raven just yet. When she opened the barn door, the three horses, a mare named Kimmela, a stallion named Kinta and their two-year-old offspring, another mare, Achahtos, looked at her and made nodding motions.

Bernadette put her hand on Achahtos muzzle and stroked her mane. She was born almost the same time as Raven, with a distinctive star on her forehead. The name Achahtos meant star in the Cree language. The other horses whinnied in protest at Bernadette's affection for Achahtos. She had to walk to the other stalls and give each of them attention.

The barn door opened. Harvey Mawer walked in. "I thought you might be in here."

"Hey Harvey, I'm visiting the horses before I turn in. How are you?"

He picked up a bucket, shook in some hay flake and offered it to the horses. "Oh, I'm fine. At my age, I find sleep to be overrated. I often come out here to visit the horses and spend time with them."

"Doesn't Ava mind you are wandering around the barn-yard at night?"

Harvey shrugged. "I've been single all my life. Ava and I have been together for only a year, and she's almost fifteen years younger than me. I hope she gets used to my strange ways."

They stroked the horses in silence. They'd known each other for several years before he'd moved into the carriage house behind them as a joint owner of the acreage. He was now pushing 80, still upright and active, but he had slowed down in the past year. For many years, Bernadette had sat with Harvey and her German Shepherd, Sprocket, as they discussed the world or let a comfortable silence fold around them.

"I guess I need to go in," Bernadette said.

"Yeah, get yourself some rest. I'll stay with the horses longer," Harvey said. He put his large hand on her shoulder and smiled.

Bernadette walked up to the house. She could see Raven's room was dark. A feeling of guilt settled in her stomach. As she opened the door, the smell of food hit her, and she remembered she hadn't eaten for hours.

Chris came out of the kitchen with a smile. "I bet you forgot to eat, or if you did, it was bad."

Bernadette folded into Chris's arms and put her head on his massive chest. "My first day at work, and I blew it."

"Did you solve a case?" Chris asked as he guided her to

the kitchen. "I saved you some chicken cacciatore and mushroom risotto I made for dinner. I kept it warm for you."

She fell into a kitchen chair as Chris put the plate in front of her. "How did Raven take me being away?"

"All she talked about was how her Mommy was a hero, going to battle bad guys. She walked around the house waving a wooden spoon. Sprocket and Pepper followed her at a distance in case she smacked them."

"I'm glad she took my absence so well."

Chris came behind her and massaged her shoulders. "How are you taking it?"

"I've got enough guilt coursing through my veins to put my heart into cardiac arrest," Bernadette said. She placed her hand on Chris's. "Can we do this?"

"You mean, can you be a detective in serious crimes division and do your job effectively while we keep our family together? We're tougher than we think. It's a matter of keeping our communication going. If that stops, then we'll need to consider our options."

Bernadette stood up and kissed Chris hard on the lips. "How did I find someone like you?"

"Didn't you tell me you'd annoyed every other man you ever dated, and I was the only one who could handle your madness?" Chris said with a laugh.

"Hey, I don't recall saying that—I may have implied it."

"Finish your dinner. I'll wash up, and you get some sleep. Do you have an early start tomorrow?"

"I meet with Durham at 7:30 a.m. We've issued an APB on a suspect, Kaitlin Godwin from HR, and deployed a CSI team to search an apartment we discovered that could be linked to the death of Eric Chan."

"Sounds like you have a busy day. I'm making a salmon

pot pie tomorrow night; it was Raven's special request. She asked me to make it because she knows it is one of your favorites."

"I'll try to be home for dinner, I promise," Bernadette said.

She finished dinner, kissed Chris, and headed upstairs. Raven's room was beside theirs. She glanced through the door and saw her sleeping, so she quietly entered, kissed Raven's forehead, and fixed her blankets.

Sprocket's enormous head rose from the opposite end of the bed. Pepper, the cat, peeked out from the foot of the crib. They had become her guardians. Sprocket had left Bernadette's bedside soon after Raven was born and Pepper, the wild barn cat that had come with the two original rescue horses in the barn, had moved in shortly afterward.

They followed her everywhere. Now that Raven was walking, Sprocket walked in front of her to clear the way, and the cat followed behind. Bernadette wondered if it was because Raven dropped so much food on the floor, but when Raven ventured outside, they were her stalwart companions.

She left Raven's room and entered the master bathroom and took a quick shower. When she returned to the bedroom, Chris was already there, snoring quietly.

The house creaked. The wind rattled tree branches against the window. There was no more comfortable place she could imagine than right here with her husband, child, menageries of pets and animals and her good friend's next door.

She fell into a peaceful sleep and never heard someone climb the steps and try the handle on the front door.

Sprocket and Pepper had heard the intruder and

watched the man from the other side of the door. Sprocket didn't make a sound. Had he entered, the dog would have lunged. Pepper extended herself as high as she could reach. Her tail was rigid and swishing rapidly; a low growl emanated from her throat. Her eyes had latched onto the man's face as a landing zone if he entered the house.

The man turned and walked away. Sprocket and Pepper watched him until he disappeared out into the lights of the yard. The snow covered his tracks.

Chapter Eleven

Raven bounded on Bernadette as her phone alarm chimed 6 a.m. "Mommy, Mommy, I'm awake, are you?"

Bernadette's eyes sprung open as her arms surrounded the little bundle of joy that landed on her. "Of course, I am now. Thanks for waking me up, sweetie," she said, holding Raven in a bear hug and sitting upright.

"I missed you, Mommy," Raven said.

"I missed you too, sweetie," Bernadette said.

"Will you chase evil men today?"

"Yes, that's my job," Bernadette said, pushing Raven's hair out of her eyes.

"I will help you someday," Raven said.

Chris walked into the bedroom and picked up Raven. "Let Mommy get into the bathroom, and then you can play with her downstairs."

Raven jumped off the bed. Sprocket and Pepper were immediately by her side as they escorted her down the stairs.

Bernadette sat up in bed and watched Raven toddle off with the pets. "How did we raise such a bright child?"

Chris watched Raven move down the stairs while holding onto the fur of Sprocket, with Pepper on the other side to steady her. "My mother told me I could hardly talk until three. This kid seems to push the boundaries."

Bernadette got dressed and checked her cell phone for messages as she brushed her hair. The crime scene investigation team would be in the apartment Chadha had said was rented by Godwin and used for hookups with Armand Paradis by 8 a.m. this morning. They'd be doing a complete sweep for fingerprints and search for drugs.

She checked herself in the mirror. "Oh my, that can't be accurate, those bags under my eyes look like I'm 90!" With a deep sigh, she opened a drawer, pulled out some concealer and applied as much as possible so she didn't look like she'd fallen out of bed.

They would meet to discuss the case. Two suspects claimed the other had been responsible for Chan's death. The truth would lie somewhere between.

One suspect, Kaitlin Godwin, was gone, as in possibly fled the scene. As Bernadette put enough concealer around her eyes to make them look less scary, she wondered where this case was going and if they'd ever bring Armand Paradis or Hanna Winter to justice.

She descended the stairs and played with Raven while Chris made pancakes. The home smelled lovely. As she looked around the kitchen, she wondered why she would leave this cocoon of happiness to work as a police officer in the world of crime. She knew the answer, so other women could enjoy this as well.

Bernadette shared her pancakes with Raven as they

discussed what they would do for the day. Raven wondered about Bernadette's battles with bad men.

"Bad men seem to be Raven's theme," Chris said as he poured Bernadette more coffee.

"Yeah, she's a bit fixated on that. Who knows, maybe she'll grow into a super crime fighter in the future," Bernadette said.

"I hope she does it by becoming a lawyer," Chris said with a smile.

Bernadette poured coffee into her to-go mug and put on her jacket, hugged and kissed Raven goodbye. "I'll text you if I'm going to be late. I really hope to keep to a regular schedule today."

"Hey, Harvey, Ava and I have you covered. You've got the weekend off; we can have some family time then. There's more snow in the forecast for Friday; we could take Raven for a sleigh ride."

Bernadette kissed Chris and headed for the door. She stopped when she noticed Sprocket and Pepper hovering close to Raven. "Have you noticed how protective the pets are of Raven this morning?"

Chris looked at Sprocket and Pepper. "Let me call Sprocket. Come over here, boy; I've got a treat for you." He held out his hand with a piece of bacon.

Sprocket didn't budge. He glanced at Raven, who played on the floor. He licked his lips toward the bacon and focused on Raven.

Chris stared at Bernadette. "That is odd behavior."

"Looks like Raven has the pets under her spell. I better get to work," Bernadette said.

She headed out the door, fired up the Jeep and got on her hands-free phone to the sergeant on duty for an update on the A.P.B. on Godwin.

"There's been no sign of her," the sergeant said.

Bernadette drove to the RCMP Detachment, parked her Jeep, and walked into the Serious Crime Unit. Evanston was sitting at her desk with a coffee, punching keys on her computer. She wasn't fast on the keyboard, more of a hunt-and-peck typist.

Evanston looked up as Bernadette walked in. "Durham delayed our meetup. He's in with the Crown Prosecutor. I'm not sure how good our case is to investigate Paradis Transport for Human Trafficking."

"Why is that?" Bernadette said as she sat beside Evanston with a coffee.

"Because that's exactly what Durham said when he left here to have breakfast with Dunwoody in the Crown's office," Evanston said.

"Damn, I thought we had something."

"Durham said he'd have a hard time proving the shipping containers sent to Canada held trafficked humans. He said he'd try to make it happen."

"Who's on point today at the Crown's office?" Bernadette asked.

"I think it's Quinn Sambora."

"I don't remember her. Is she new?"

"Right out of law school, and a real stickler for the law. We'll need hard evidence from the apartment."

Durham walked into the room and motioned to Bernadette and Evanston to come to his office. They entered and found him sitting and running his hand over his bald head in his nervous tick fashion.

"What's the word?" Bernadette asked.

"Unless we find something in the apartment Chadha mentioned, you have nothing more than hearsay from Chadha. Without Godwin or Paradis prints, no leads exist."

"I just pulled a guy off his flight to India, received a complete confession of his supposed involvement, and he put the finger on a suspect in a murder, and I've got nothing?" Bernadette asked.

"Welcome back to the police force; I'm afraid those are the breaks. I hope the C.S.I. team comes up with something today," Durham said.

Bernadette shook her head. "You mind if I visit the apartment this morning with the C.S.I. team?"

"Go ahead, but there are four other cases I need you to look at, so hurry back," Durham said.

Chapter Twelve

Armand Paradis looked over the Red Deer River Valley from the picture window of his mansion and drank his double espresso with extra hot foam. An hour had passed since the sun rose, but no word had reached him from his contact.

His phone rang. "Hello, who is it?"

"It's me, Franco. It didn't go well last night."

"I realize that. There would have been police and ambulance sirens all night if you'd had the guts to take that bitch Bernadette Callahan out last night. What happened?"

"A big dog and a nasty-looking cat guarded the front door," Franco said.

"Did either of these terrifying pets have a gun?"

"No, they didn't have a gun. Why do you ask?"

"Then why didn't you shoot them? Did you not have a silencer on your gun? Why didn't you use it?"

"The door was locked. I could have opened it in thirty seconds, but the dog would have barked and woken up Callahan and her husband. She is a police officer and probably had a gun. I didn't go there for a shoot-out; I intended to murder them in their beds."

"I wonder why you didn't think of this before you took the job. And here Detective Callahan is, alive and causing me a headache," Armand said.

"Hey, I told you, when you hand me a contract, the target is as good as dead. Now that I understand the layout, I'll be ready next time," Franco said.

Armand drained his espresso and placed it on the polished mahogany table with the gold inlay. "I expect you to do your job, Franco." He put his phone down and turned toward the door as his wife, Sofia, entered.

"What's the problem? You seem upset," Sofia said.

Armand composed himself. Sofia was his wife of thirty years. They'd been together since they left Montreal. The death of their two sons years ago shattered her mental state. He needed to be careful not to upset her with his business dealings and his extra-marital affairs.

"It's nothing, my dear. I'm trying to get our roof tiles fitted with snow breakers. I don't want to see the snow slide off the roof onto your lovely car when you pull out of the driveway,"

Armand said.

Sofia gave Armand a hug. "You are so thoughtful, Armand. What would I do without you?"

"You'd find yourself in the arms of one of the young men who service our swimming pool in Maui," Armand said with a wink.

"Oh, you are so funny. But speaking of Maui, when shall we go? The weather is turning frightfully cold next week. I don't want to get trapped at the airport trying to escape."

"That's a splendid idea, my dear. Why don't you go this

week, and I'll follow you. There's a pile of work I need to finish, but I don't want to bore you with it while we're away."

Sofia smiled. "Well, if you insist." She whirled and waved to him over her shoulder. "You know I'll miss you terribly on the beach. I'm going to book a business class flight and pack my bags."

Armand watched her walk out of the room. He loved her dearly, but he could not keep his hands off younger women. Hanna Winter had been his downfall several years ago, and so had Kaitlin Godwin. He berated himself for having affairs with women in the office, but he couldn't help himself. He reminded himself, "I am French and a man, what can I do?"

He grabbed his phone and dialed Felicity Haynsworth. "You understand, I can't discuss Chadha's case with you," she said when she answered.

"How much time do I have before the police come to investigate my business and cause me distress?" Armand asked.

Haynsworth paused before she spoke. "You want me to be disbarred?"

"You must have learned some rumors while you were there last night?"

"Okay, there's a rumor of the Canadian Security and Intelligence Service becoming involved."

"And they are?" Armand asked.

"Oh my God, Armand, have you been living under a rock? They are like the FBI in the USA with similar powers. Once they get involved, you can kiss your business goodbye. And the lawyer you need won't be me at a paltry five hundred per hour."

"I love it when you talk money, makes me horny. Sofia is

leaving for Maui tomorrow. Why don't you drop by my apartment downtown?" Armand asked.

"So cute, Armand, I think I've given you enough sexual favors over the years—"

"And you've billed accordingly," Armand countered.

"Well, here's some news for you. The little apartment you've been using for all your trysts will crawl with police this morning. Chadha gave it up last night."

"Damn," Armand said.

"And it gets better, and this will definitely be the talk of the town in seventy-two hours," Felicity said with a chuckle in her voice. "Chadha claims Kaitlin Godwin was behind Chan's murder."

"How can that be?"

"You'll find out in discovery when they bring Chadha to court at 9 am."

"He's going to give everyone up?" Armand asked in disbelief.

"Yes, my rumor mill tells me that your ex-accountant threw many of his previous work colleagues under the bus."

"Have the police arrested Kaitlin?"

"She's gone."

"Gone? I did not know she was leaving," Armand said.

"Of course you didn't. She claims she is carrying your child. Are you aware you are the father?"

"What! Impossible," Armand shouted on the phone.

"No, my dear, it can be possible. You've always been so cavalier about no protection during sex. Did you think every woman you had sex with was taking precautions? Kaitlin Godwin clearly had an infatuation with you. Now, she has a baby. And she can bring not only your business down but your entire life. Imagine what will happen when your wife finds out?"

Armand clenched his jaws as he listened. After a long pause, he said, "I'll call you when I need your help."

He quickly dialed a number. "Franco, I have another contract for you. Drop the one I just gave you and get on this one right away."

"Who is it?"

"Kaitlin Godwin. Find her and keep her away from the police."

Chapter Thirteen

Bernadette drove to the Valley Ridge Apartments that Kaitlin Godwin and Armand Paradis used for meet-ups. The place had police tape and two crime scene investigators in full white Tyvek coveralls with gloves and booties going over the place.

The apartment had been built in the late nineties, renovated several times by various corporate owners and recently painted with a massive mural on the street side. Bernadette wondered if Chan had time to admire the valley before he plunged to his death.

She found the lead investigator, Enrique Sanchez; he was late twenties with short hair and a slight mustache. "Any information on the residents here?"

Sanchez shook his head. "I checked with the apartment manager, Zoe Javernick. This unit is supposed to be a guest suite for the use of the entire building, but I had officers canvas the other tenants. No one knew it existed."

"That's very convenient. Hide a 'hook-up pad' in plain

sight. No sign-in sheet for using the apartment, then?" Bernadette asked.

"There's nothing. The manager possessed a set of keys for the place. Despite regular cleaning, the building manager never knew who used the apartment. She assumed it was a perk for the employees of Armand's business."

"Sounds like it got a lot of use from what I heard," Bernadette said. "Did your team find any fingerprints?"

"Yes, but I have a feeling they will match the cleaners. The place is spotless. I wish I had these people clean my place," Sanchez said.

"Make sure you check all the drains in the sinks, shower, and bathtub for chemical residue. If you get anything, have the coroner do a cross-match with what we found in Eric Chan's autopsy," Bernadette said.

"Noted, Detective. I'll make sure everything goes to the coroner if we get something," Sanchez replied.

Bernadette walked into the living room and let her eyes sweep over the designer furniture, artwork and rugs. A wine fridge caught her attention; she opened it and looked inside.

"This wine fridge is fully stocked," Bernadette said to the officer beside her. She made her way back to the building manager's office. "Who orders the wine for that apartment?"

Zoe Javernick looked up with a surprised look on her face. "Oh, the wine. Yes, that's right, I think it's the one uptown. They bring it in, and I have my maintenance man put it in their wine bar. There's a local deli that brings in food, but that's only on rare occasions. I think the guests bring their own with them."

"You've seen no one coming or going into that apartment?"

The manager shook her head. She was a middle-aged

woman with purple highlights in her hair and large fake eyelashes. Her large lashes fluttered now as she spoke. "I've been told that the apartment was none of my business."

"Who told you that?"

"The manager who previously held this job, his name was Jacob Kirlew. He's gone now, retired to Florida a year ago, then had a heart attack and died. Not that old either, kind of a shame."

"Yes, sorry to hear about that," Bernadette said, although not sure how to give condolences for someone the manager hardly knew. She wrote a note regarding the ex-manager and to find out who had the final say over the building in the Paradis group of companies. It had to be Armand Paradis, but he would be hard to pin down.

She tried to find a connection to human trafficking and Armand's company two years back. He'd gone ballistic and called the city's mayor to shut her investigation down. The mayor had called the superintendent of her division. Armand's ploy worked. They put her on paid leave, and she took an additional year off to care for her child.

Now, things were different. There was a new mayor in town, the superintendent had retired, and Armand Paradis had few friends in the police force in his corner. As for Bernadette Callahan, Armand and his company were fair game.

Chapter Fourteen

Armand Paradis looked at his watch. He couldn't remember what time Chadha was being arraigned before a judge. Had they begun proceedings against him based on Chadha's testimony?

He picked up the phone and made a phone call and dreaded the voice on the other line. He knew she would be mad as hell.

"What is it?" Hanna Winter asked.

"The police picked up Chadha last night, and Godwin has made a run for it. I think she implicated him in Chan's death, and then he implicated her," he said with a catch in his voice.

"I thought Chadha had left for India?" Hanna said.

"He wasn't fast enough. I told him that Detective Callahan would be trouble the moment she returned to duty."

"Did you tell him in person or text him?"

"I told him in person, of course. Do you think I'm stupid?"

"That remains to be seen. Why would Godwin make a run for it?" Hanna asked.

"She seems to think she's carrying my child, and I think she might have seen me with Chan the night he committed suicide."

"Oh my, you really are stupid," Hanna said with a laugh. "How can you be so silly as to involve yourself with a person from your office? Wasn't she involved in Chan's dismissal?"

"Well, yes, she was, but there was a clear-cut case of fraud," Armand said.

Hanna laughed. "I can't believe you, Armand. You wrote the script for Chan's death, and you believe in the fiction of suicide."

"But I was never there at the time. The coroner claimed Chan jumped to his death. I gave that in my testimony."

"Never mind. What would a thorough police search uncover? Will they discover any documents pertaining to our special shipments?"

"There shouldn't be, no wait, there were the special refits that Chan saw. But I deleted the documents," Armand said with satisfaction.

"Armand, deleting something on a computer does not delete it. A forensic police expert can recover it unless you hit trash and overwrite the file. I can't believe you didn't run the operation from Bucharest like I told you," Hanna said.

"And deal with the Romanian Mafia?" Armand said with disgust.

"They are easier to deal with than the police. Now listen. We have a week to move twelve containers from Hamburg. Leave Canada immediately and catch a flight to Frankfurt tonight, then connect to Venice."

"Why not to Hamburg?"

"Because you're heading to Venice to meet a contact for the containers," Hanna said.

"Why wouldn't I fly directly to Venice?"

"*Auch mein got.* Stop being an *imbecile*! If you fly to your destination, they will track you. You fly into Frankfurt, then make a cash payment for a flight to Venice. Am I understood?"

"Yes, of course. I understand. I'll let my wife know about an urgent business matter. Will you be flying there as well?"

"I'm in Venice now at the Hilton Hotel; I'll see you when you get here."

Armand put his phone down, went into the home's massive walk-in closet that was as big as a one-bedroom apartment and began packing. He called his secretary while he threw clothes into his bag. Diedre Frank had been with him for years. She was mid-forties, attractive and capable. She was one of the few women in his company that he had not tried to sleep with because he needed her to keep his other affairs on track.

"Diedre, I need a plane ticket to Venice tonight, no sorry, that's to Frankfurt," Armand said.

"Oh, Venice sounds so much better than Frankfurt," Diedre said.

"Damn it, you're right. Make it to Venice. I don't want to wait around."

"First Class or business?"

"First Class, I hate being stuffed into those seats in business class. I love those pods in first class."

Diedre got on her computer. "There's no first class available today. I can get you on tomorrow morning at 7 a.m., and book you into a hotel tonight at the Calgary Airport. Would that be, okay?"

"Book me my usual room at the Marriott," Armand said.

"Done. I'll send you all your confirmations and your boarding pass. Anything else, Mr. Paradis?"

"No, inform the office I'll be gone for a few days, tell them I'm in Frankfurt if they ask," Armand said. He placed one of his finest jackets in the suitcase, along with several of what he considered his sexiest shirt. Hanna Winter may be fearful on the phone, but she was great in bed. He looked forward to cleaning up this business of human cargo and being done with this type of transport forever.

Chapter Fifteen

Bernadette Callahan was restless. She didn't want to return to the division. If she did, there'd be reports or other cases to review. This was the hunt, and she knew what to do. Yesterday's fishing expedition to Paradis Transport had flushed out Godwin and Chadha, but she needed something more - a link to Armand Paradise.

She rolled up on Paradis Transport, called in that she was at an interview, and walked into the reception. A young lady behind the desk named Jamila asked how she could help.

"My name is Detective Bernadette Callahan of the Police Serious Crimes Division. I'd like a few moments with Diedre Frank, Mr. Armand Paradis's personal secretary, please."

Jamila's eyes became visibly larger, and she quickly dialed the phone. "Ms. Frank, there's a detective here to see you."

"It's Callahan, and I'll tell her I'll only need a minute."

"Ah, her name is Callahan, and she'll only need a

minute," Jamila said, darting her eyes up at Bernadette and back to her phone. "It's fine. Take the right stairs. She'll meet you there."

Bernadette thanked her and strolled up the stairs, intending to draw out the tension that Diedre must be feeling. Personal secretaries knew things about their bosses that no one else would know. Bernadette intended to pry that loose.

Deidre greeted Bernadette with a firm handshake. "How may I help you, detective?"

"I have a few questions about your company's apartment in the center of the city," Bernadette said.

"Oh, what apartment would that be?" Deidre asked with a raised eyebrow.

Bernadette focused on Deidre. She was an older woman, perhaps in her late forties, with silver highlights, designer glasses and wearing an expensive designer dress. Bernadette noticed Diedre was well-compensated and would be reluctant to reveal her secrets.

"I'm here to investigate the apartment in the Valley View Towers that this company owns. The apartment was one floor below Eric Chan's."

"Oh, we so miss Eric, his death was so unexpected and horrible."

"Yes, Diedre, it was. Now, let's talk about the apartment. How often did you ship wine and food there, and who ordered it?" Bernadette asked.

"I don't know what you're talking about," Diedre said, sitting back at her desk.

"I can get a warrant to search every delivery you've made to that apartment. I'm guessing you're the one that set up the apartment for Mr. Paradis."

Diedre paused and shook her head. "I'm just a secretary.

I look after Mr. Paradis's personal files, communication, and his travel."

"That's wonderful, but let me make it clear to you: if the apartment we are investigating contains any evidence we can link to the death of Eric Chan, you become an accessory."

"How could that be? Eric committed suicide."

"Someone assisted him over the balcony, which we classify as murder," Bernadette said. "I really don't want to cause you alarm, but anything you can do to assist us…"

"Murder! I can't believe anyone would want to murder Eric."

"Really? They accused him of theft of thousands of dollars. Does anyone here hold a grudge against him?"

"I've been with this company for a long time, detective. I don't know of anyone who might want to harm him."

"Or perhaps they had someone else, do it? Did you hear of any office banter or getting even with Eric?'"

Diedre straightened up and stared hard at Bernadette. "Our employees are loyal to the company, our president and each other. This is one of the best companies to work for in the county."

"I'm happy to hear that. You must enjoy a lot of perks."

"Yes, we do," Diedre said with a smile.

"I imagine access to the special apartment must be one of them," Bernadette said. She paused and waited for Diedre to flinch.

"Ah, well, not exactly."

There it was. The tone in her voice changed. Bernadette tried not to smile. No one could hide something forever. Now, she had to tread carefully.

"Who used the apartment?" Bernadette asked quietly.

"I would have to check. Just give me a day or two."

"I can get a search warrant for your files within an hour if I leave now. Officers will tear every inch of your perfectly put-together office apart to find information regarding access to the apartment," Bernadette said.

She watched Diedre stiffen; her bottom lip trembled.

"Or you could just give me a list of names right now, and I promise I'll be out of here. Would that be more suitable?"

"Yes, very suitable," Diedre said. She whirled to her computer, opened a file, and sent it to her printer. Within a minute, Bernadette received a file with three names.

Bernadette looked at the file. "Kaitlin Godwin, Sanjay Chadha and Armand Paradis are the only ones who had access to the apartment."

"Yes, that is correct."

"And they all had their own keys?"

"Kaitlin told me they used a scheduling app to book when they wanted the apartment. I was told in advance if anyone wanted food and refreshments delivered." Deidre said.

"How often was the apartment used?"

"I wouldn't know. I have a master key, but I've never been there, and I've never been privy to the scheduling app," Diedre said.

Bernadette took notes and looked up. "Do you know how they enter the apartment garage?"

"I'm not sure. They must have an access code of some kind," Diedre replied.

"You don't know what those access codes would be, do you?"

Diedre shook her head. "No, I've never been there. They make all deliveries to the main entrance, and the staff sends them upstairs at the manager's request."

Bernadette closed her notepad. "Thank you, you've most helpful. But there's one more thing I wanted to ask you."

"What is that?"

"Where is Armand Paradis? Is he still in town? I only want to ask a few simple questions, and I promise I won't take up too much of his time."

"Oh, I'm sure he wouldn't mind, but he's off on a business trip to Germany," Diedre said.

"I hope it's somewhere nice. I hear the Christmas markets open in Germany soon," Bernadette said.

"Well, he is going to Frankfurt, but then on to Venice—oops, I wasn't supposed to say that," Diedre said, holding her hand to her mouth.

"I'm sure that's fine. We in the police department are good at keeping secrets," Bernadette said with a wink.

"I think he's afraid the staff will get jealous of his exotic travels."

"Venice in late November will be cold, but fewer tourists, so I'm sure he'll enjoy the sights when he's able to take time off work. When did he leave?"

"Oh, he hasn't left yet. He had our limousine drive him to the Calgary airport. I got him his favorite hotel room, and he's off bright and early at 7 a.m."

Bernadette thanked Diedre and went to her car. She fired up the engine and turned on the seat heaters. She took only a few seconds to access the flight to Frankfurt and the corresponding connection to Venice.

There wasn't much time. She knew it was impossible for them to get Interpol to shadow Paradis in Venice, but there was one person who could. Bernadette dialed her number and hoped she was there.

Chapter Sixteen

"Hello, who is this?" a woman with a German accent answered.

"It's me, Bernadette Callahan, is that Katriona Sager?"

"Yah, and you know I preferred to be called Kat. What's up?"

Bernadette laughed. "It's good to hear your voice, Kat. We haven't talked for almost a year." Kat Sager was a former B.K.A. officer in the German police, a division like the American F.B.I. She was in her early thirties, medium height, dark hair, blue eyes, single and strong willed.

"How is your daughter, Raven and your good-looking husband, Chris? He is still bulging with the muscles and cooking for you?" Kat asked.

"They are great. But I'm calling to ask you a favor, but first, I must ask where you are right now?"

"I'm in Berlin. Why do you ask?"

"Armand Paradis is heading to Venice, and he's changing planes in Frankfurt. I'm investigating his company.

We think he's come up with a new plan to refit shipping containers for humans out of Hamburg."

"I've heard rumors about this. Karl Steiner has been monitoring human traffickers lately. They told us there was a big shipment coming soon. Someone wants to move high-priced prostitutes by special fitted containers to North America," Kat said.

"Can I ask if you put these human traffickers in jail or in the ground?" Bernadette asked.

"You can ask, but I won't tell you. I told you some time ago I'm tired of the legal system. My grandfather left me an inheritance that allows me to do what I want. I hunt criminals now. What I do with them when I find them is my business."

Bernadette took a breath. "I should not have asked you that question. I apologize; you're right, it's none of my business. But I hope if you help me track Armand, you will leave him in one piece. If you could find out who he is meeting in Venice, we might find out more about his human trafficking operations."

"I'd love to. What time does his plane arrive in Frankfurt?" Kat asked.

"I'll text you the information. Let me know who he contacts. You might see Hanna Winter there."

"She's the one I'd shoot without hesitation."

"See if you can control yourself," Bernadette said.

"Only for you. I will do it for you, Bernadette, and for Raven."

"Thank you. I appreciate it." Bernadette ended her call and wondered about Kat Sager. Two years ago, they worked on a cold case that brought them together. Kat flew to Canada to track Hanna Winter, the alleged head of a human trafficking gang from Germany. Winter had threatened Kat's mother and sent someone to kill Kat. Her partner got hurt while she escaped injuries. After freeing twenty hostages held by the traffickers and an almost fatal meeting with Winter, Kat had searched for Winter but couldn't find her.

Bernadette realized their paths had crossed again. Katriona Sager was similar in temperament and instinct to her own, but with a difference: Kat was more reckless. And now, she no longer worked within the limits of the law.

Chapter Seventeen

Kat Sager checked the schedule of Armand's Lufthansa flight from Calgary with a connection through Toronto that would arrive at 9:30 am. There were several hours of layovers until the flight to Venice at 1 pm. Why Paradis had booked that flight was a mystery. He could have flown directly to Venice via Toronto, but that didn't matter to her.

She packed a bag and booked a morning flight from Berlin to Frankfurt. Her flight would arrive one hour before his. She booked the flight to Venice in the economy as she knew from dealing with Armand in the past that his ego would not let him travel in anything less than business or first class. But she chose a seat in the first row of economy. That way, she could monitor Armand.

The next morning, she was at the airport in a red wig, dark leather jacket, casual sweater, jeans, and a cheap carry-on bag. Her plane was on time. It landed one hour before Armand's plane from Canada.

With an iPad on her lap, she sat in a waiting area off to one side and made sure she had her eyes down as Armand strutted out of his plane, gliding his bag beside him. Kat dropped into step far enough behind him to remain out of his sight. She intended to confirm he wasn't leaving the airport.

He entered the business class lounge, and Kat found a seat outside the lounge and waited. The many years she had spent in the German police force taught her the essence of surveillance was patience. She sent a text to Karl Steiner, who was already in Venice. He'd be waiting at the airport with a car.

Steiner had taken on the role of her mentor in the fine art of tracking humans for the past two years. They formed a bond after successfully rescuing twenty human trafficking victims from a mansion in Calgary, Canada.

Kat Sager developed a desire to operate independently, free from the constraints of law enforcement, the legal system, and strict adherence to regulations. Before the wall fell, the East German Stasi police had employed Steiner. He'd been a spy and assassin for the Communist Party.

Karl Steiner informed her about a sizable inheritance from her grandfather. She couldn't go back to being a cop once she started. With Steiner by her side, they tracked down high-level criminals, leaders of gangs and drug lords. Some they gave to the police; others received a quick death.

They called it the 'brass verdict' when the criminal seemed so vile there was no recourse. A bullet was their judgment call. Now, she would decide what Armand Paradis would get once they found out who he was meeting.

Kat sent a text to Steiner that she'd made a visual of their target. He acknowledged her text and was standing by. Karl was exceptional with logistics and weapons. After he flew to Venice, a contact had provided him with two Uzi submachine guns, two Glock 17 handguns, plus an assortment of handcuffs, knives, and pepper spray. They were ready for anyone that Paradis met up with.

They'd done this drill many times before. Kat found herself a little cafe across from the business lounge, ordered a coffee, and checked her watch. Paradis had just one hour left before needing to leave for the flight.

Paradis sat in the business lounge, ordered a beer, and chose some items from the food bar. He was hungry. Although he'd just had breakfast on the plane of eggs benedict, croissants, and fruit, he needed to nibble on something to settle his stomach.

He always ate when he was nervous. The tone in Hanna Winter's voice made him uneasy. He'd never met her associates as his role had been pure operations. When Hanna asked for changed shipping containers, he provided them. That the containers transported humans being trafficked for prostitution or any menial slave labor did not bother him.

Armand had been at arm's length in every transaction. He'd made sure nothing came back to him; now, that was impossible. His hand trembled as he raised his beer to his lips. He put the glass down and steadied himself. A server came by and asked him in English if Armand needed anything else.

"Yes, a tall scotch with no ice and water on the side," Armand replied to the server.

The server returned with his drink. Armand took a large sip and set it down. "I will need two more of these. I'm a bit of a nervous flyer," Armand said, pushing his long, wavy gray hair from his forehead.

His cell phone buzzed with a text from Hanna Winter. *"I hope you've made it to Frankfurt. Were you able to get a flight to Venice?"*

Hanna's text made Armand sweat even more. She'd given him strict instructions to fly only to Frankfurt, leave the airport and pay cash for a flight to Venice. He'd done none of that. If anyone wanted to know his whereabouts, he'd left an obvious trail.

The second scotch kicked in. Now, he didn't care. He was halfway through his third when he noticed it was time to board his plane. Downing the last of his scotch, he pulled himself from the deep leather lounge chair and pushed his feet toward the exit.

He stopped at the door of the executive lounge, ran his hand over his hair, and smoothed his jacket. With a shake of his head, he reminded himself he was Armand Paradis, one of the richest men in his city. It was a little city of just over one hundred thousand, but he was the richest, and in his alcohol-infused state, that thought made him smile.

Kat Sager watched Armand exit the lounge and noticed his body seemed to list to one side as if a ship had taken on too much ballast or struck an iceberg. Following him would not be hard.

He rolled up to the airport check-in desk, presented his passport and boarding pass with a flourish and took steps as if he was walking on air. The passenger service agent watched Armand with interest for a moment, then turned to help another passenger check in.

Kat knew that had Armand been flying economy, someone might have denied him boarding. Money had its privilege.

The service agent called for Kat's zone to board. She walked on the plane, pulling her roller bag with her iPad in front of her face, and checking her seat number. Armand was in his seat, nursing a scotch with a bemused look on his face. He never looked up.

Kat took her seat behind the business class bulkhead and watched Armand. He slurped his scotch and dropped his head. The plane taxied, accelerated on the runway, and lifted off.

Once they gained altitude, the flight attendant closed the curtain between business and economy. Kat downloaded Lufthansa's wireless app and texted Steiner that their target was very drunk.

Steiner replied, "We need to be careful following him."

Chapter Eighteen

The plane landed at the Marco Polo Airport, just fourteen kilometers from Venice. The flight crew pulled back the curtain between first class and economy for landing. Kat watched Armand Paradis wake from his slumber and comb his hair.

She was worried he'd be too drunk and need help to get off the aircraft. Much to her surprise, Armand straightened his jacket and walked off the plane. The passengers collected their overhead luggage, and Kat followed Armand off the airplane.

Steiner had said there were many options Armand could take from the airport. The first was a car to the outskirts of Venice, then a water taxi. Or, he could have a private water taxi take him to his hotel from a dock near the airport.

Kat's assignment was to mark which direction Armand headed from the arrivals hall. Steiner would wait there with several accomplices at points that Armand could veer off to.

They needed to know the hotel Armand was staying at to find out who he was meeting.

The next ten minutes would be important. Kat followed at a safe distance behind Armand and couldn't help noticing his walk had an unsteady gait. He leaned on his roller bag and stopped, then turned around.

Kat grabbed a map from her bag and put her face in it. Did he know he was being followed?

Armand walked toward her. There was nothing she could do—she couldn't stand there; it would look too obvious. She walked by Armand without glancing at him.

When she got a few hundred meters away, she turned back toward Armand. He wasn't there.

Kat ran back down the hallway. There were signs in Italian and English not to stop, alarm could be set off. Her heart raced. Where had he gone?

Turning a corner, she almost collided with him. Armand was picking up a paper with his itinerary.

"*Mi scusi signore*," Kat blurted out. She looked up at the exit sign. "*Ah, sto andando nella direzione sbagliata.*"

"I don't speak Italian," Armand muttered.

"I'm going the wrong way," Kat replied with a smile.

Armand took Kat by the arm. "Yes, this is the way out; let me escort such a beautiful lady."

"This is your first time in Venice?" Kat asked.

Armand stared into Kat's blue eyes. "Yes, never been here before, and you?"

"My mother lives here. I'm going to visit her." Kat lied and hoped her fake Italian accent was working. She'd taken two years of Italian lessons in university and found the language easy to learn.

"Ah, it's so sad I'm only here for a few days. I'd love to see the city with a lovely lady like you."

Kat winked at him. "Thank you for your kind words. Perhaps I can drop by for a drink. What hotel are you staying at?"

Armand looked at the piece of paper he'd retrieved from the ground. "I'm staying at the Hilton Molino, Stucky? Is that correct?"

"Yes, that is correct, the Hilton Molino Stucky. Your reservation states a private water taxi will take you there."

Armand looked impressed. "That's nice, why don't you give me your number? Perhaps you can show me your lovely city."

"Perhaps you can give me your number, signore. I'll call you if I'm available."

Armand passed his phone to her. "Of course, here it is."

She copied his number. "Now, I must go. My mother is waiting for me." Kat disappeared into the crowd of people waiting for arrivals.

Steiner was standing there in shock as she left Armand. "How did that happen?"

"Short story. His drunken stupor almost blew my cover. I have the name of his hotel. All we need to do is watch it to see who he contacts."

"He gave you the name of his hotel?"

"Yes, and his phone number. He's a lecherous old man, he wants a 'booty call' while he's here on business," Kat said with a sneer.

Steiner watched Armand over Kat's shoulder. "I'm certain about the lecherous, but I don't take his word about where he's going. Let's watch him."

Kat turned to see two men approach Armand. They stood on either side; one took his bag, and they marched him out of the arrivals hall.

"You see the surprise on Armand's face?"

"Yes, he wasn't expecting them. We need to follow him, now!" Kat said.

Chapter Nineteen

Steiner and Kat followed the men, taking Armand Paradis out of the airport. They hurried him to the curb, where a black BMW sedan screeched to a halt. They shoved Armand into the back and sat on either side of him.

The sedan took off. Steiner spoke into his cell phone, *"Enzo, vieni, qui velocemente!"*

A black Ferrari, a four-door sedan, rolled up to the curb. Steiner opened the back door. "Let's get after him."

Kat almost fell into the luxurious back seat. Steiner jumped in beside her. *"Ezno, andare!"*

Enzo was a stocky man in a white shirt, black suit, bald head, and sunglasses, with a short, trimmed beard. Kat noticed he might be trying to channel Jason Statham but with a Ferrari sedan.

A few minutes later, they caught up to the BMW. Enzo kept the car in sight and slid in and out of traffic. The traffic was light on the freeway toward Venice.

Steiner checked his phone. "I ran the license plate of

the car. It's a rental. I doubt the guys with Armand are from the Hilton Hotel."

"Any idea where they'll take him?"

"I'm hoping it's a small hotel where we can get eyes on him."

They followed the sedan onto the causeway leading into Venice. Steiner moved forward in his seat. "I think they will stop at the Piazzale Roma, it is a bus stop and close to the water taxis. From there, it's anyone's guess where they will take him. We'll be lucky to get to a water taxi in time. Leave your bag with Enzo—we need to move fast."

"Got it," Kat said. Her heart was racing. As tough as this tracking was, she loved every minute of the chase.

Next to the quay, the sedan came to a stop. After pulling Armand out, the men grabbed his bag and headed toward a sleek wooden private water taxi. The boat was mahogany with a low cabin, leather seats and a male captain who oozed testosterone in a black leather jacket.

"Get the boat number," Steiner commanded.

Kat noted the number as the boat's engines rumbled, then roared off down the canal. They hopped into a taxi behind it, and Steiner gave instructions to follow the first taxi. The driver only smiled and expected a big tip. He loved the drama of tourists who came to Venice.

The taxi roared down the Grand Canal in the wake of the one it was following. Steiner instructed the taxi captain to "*segui lentamente,*" to follow slow. The driver smiled and moved the throttle back. His two passengers didn't resemble paid assassins. He imagined they were private detectives paid by a jealous wife to get extra money in a divorce.

A large hotel came into view. The taxi moored at its dock, unloaded the passengers and took off. The two men guided Armand between them to the front door of the hotel. They looked less ominous now and handled Armand as if he was a premium client being treated to five-star service.

Armand was quiet. He did not say a word to either of them.

Kat watched them enter the hotel, then turned to Steiner. "What do we do now?"

"That's the Monaco Hotel on Grand Canal."

"Is it as classy as the Hilton that Armand was supposed to be staying at?"

"Oh yes, three times the Hilton. But I'd love to know who he's going to meet," Steiner said.

"I have a plan," Kat said.

"What is it?"

"Let's check into the hotel, send for my bag, and I get into a disguise so we can see who he's meeting."

"But he's already met you," Steiner said.

"He met an Italian lady with red hair, and he was quite drunk. I plan to be my lovely West Berliner self with dark hair. I bet you your favorite Venetian cocktail. I can pull it off."

"You're on," Steiner said. He clicked on the hotel's app, made their reservations, and called Enzo. "We'll have our bags in an hour. Meet me in the lobby for cocktails—you're buying if I don't like your disguise."

Chapter Twenty

Armand Paradis sobered up by the time the two men thrust him into his luxurious room. They had lost their polite composure in the elevator. Neither man had spoken to him other than a few grunts and one-word commands. Armand assumed the men were from some Slavic, post-communist country and were members of a less-than-reputable gang. They were a perfect match for recruits of Hanna Winter.

The men closed the hotel door and left. Armand brushed himself off, washed his face in the bathroom, and found a bottle of scotch in the room's liquor cabinet. A moment later, the door opened. He looked up as Hanna Winter walked in.

"Ah, there you are," Armand said with as much bravado as he could muster. Hanna looked beautiful in high heels, tight leather pants, and a cream, low-cut blouse, but the scowl on her face told him he had to be careful. Hanna was thirty-seven, medium height, with an impressive figure, blonde hair, and blue eyes. She was his lover and partner in human trafficking for years. But he never knew when she'd turn from lover to ruthless businesswoman.

Hanna walked into the room, put her hand on Armand's chest, and unbuttoned his shirt. "Did you have any trouble finding the place?"

"You sent your welcoming committee. How could I miss it?"

Hanna continued unbuttoning his shirt and reached for his belt. She undid his belt and pulled down his zipper. "Tell me, did you book your flight direct to Venice after I told you not to?"

"Well, I…"

Hanna grabbed his member and squeezed. "Did you?"

"Yikes, yes, but it was my secretary, Diedre. I told her not to. But it was too late. I didn't know until I boarded the plane—you know how damned efficient she is."

Hanna relaxed her grip. "Just in case you were followed, I had those men pick you up."

"But I told no one, believe me."

Hanna squeezed again. This time, Armand yelped in pain.

"You told no one—except your secretary. Is that right?"

"Yes, only Deidre and she won't tell a soul," Armand said, hoping Hanna would relax her hold.

"What if she was forced to by a warrant? That Detective Callahan can be annoying, don't you think?" Hanna asked. Her voice became soft, and she massaged his member.

"Well, ah yes, ah, yes she can," Armand said. Her actions had taken him by surprise.

"As annoying as I can be?" Hanna said as she slid another hand down to give Armand her full attention.

"Well, now, that is not annoying at all," Armand said with his eyes rolling back in his head.

Hanna pulled her hands away and stepped back. "Good, then it's time you paid attention. You are here to do a job. Take a shower and meet me in the lobby in twenty minutes. We have a dinner meeting with our contact from Romania."

Armand shook his head and zipped up his pants. "Why are we meeting him here and not in Frankfurt?"

"His mother lives here. And it's the only time he would meet with us. Now, get changed and meet me in the lobby," Hanna said. She walked back to Armand and kissed him hard on the lips. "If you perform well tonight, I'll do a little performing for you."

Chapter Twenty-One

Steiner and Kat checked into the Hotel Monaco and went to their separate rooms. Kat entered her room and opened the balcony window to view the fabled Grand Canal. The hotel had renovated the room in blue and gold, with plush furniture and luxurious bedding. She took a moment to send a text to Bernadette Callahan to ask her if she'd found any leads from the accountant and the H.R. director at Armand's' company.

This entire day was a déjà vu to the time she'd tracked down Hanna Winter in Canada. And now, she was in Venice, back on the trail of Hanna Winter, who was once a promising student of philosophy and psychology from a small university in East Germany. They were the same age, the same middle-class German upbringing and yet, Hanna Winter had morphed into a person who trafficked humans for money.

Kat's cell phone buzzed. Bernadette Callahan texted her she might have a potential lead on who might have entered the apartment of a murder victim, she'd know more once they had a warrant. She smiled at the text. In her present life, she needed no warrants. Steiner had handed her a Glock 17 with an extra clip. That was the only warrant she needed.

She took a quick shower in the opulent marble bathroom, toweled herself dry with the plush bath towels and slipped into the scented bathrobe before answering the door to get her luggage.

The bag held the essentials of her spy kit. Two wigs, underwear, and some kick-ass clothes to make her seem like a high-class Berliner *fraulein* who didn't give a damn about what the rest of the world thought.

She pulled on tight black leather pants, a cream blouse, slipped on high-heeled boots and a black leather jacket with a large scarf that could double as a shawl or head covering. With a quick spritz of perfume, she exited her room and went downstairs to meet Steiner.

He was reclining in a chair, his long legs splayed out in faded jeans with distressed leather boots, a paisley shirt, and a brown leather jacket. His long gray hair fell over his shoulders and his manicured fingers rested in his lap as if he owned the world. Not a motion in the room missed his attention. He'd been a trained killer in his last career and had become her mentor. They had a strange bond. Sometimes, he felt like a teacher and a guide, and then, as she viewed his perfect form reclined in that chair, she fantasized about taking him to bed and riding him like a stallion.

She shook her head to break the image and approached Steiner with a smile. "Any sign of our target?"

"Not yet," Steiner said. He rose from his chair and directed Kat to the chair opposite him. A waiter approached. He placed two wine glasses with a ruby red liquid and a green olive onto a small table between them.

"What is this?" Kat asked.

Steiner leaned forward to hand her a glass. "This is a Select Spritz, two parts Venetian bitter aperitive, three parts Prosecco and a splash of soda. The olive is both a garnish and an antipasto."

Kat sipped it and smiled. "And am I buying this round?"

"You look stunning. Armand will never recognize you. I knew you'd pull it off, so I already paid for the drinks."

Kat took another sip and chewed on the olive. "I wonder if Hanna will allow Armand to roam the streets of Venice or if she'll keep him here—"

Steiner looked behind Kat as the elevator door opened. "Looks like they just arrived. Cover your head!"

Chapter Twenty-Two

Kat pulled the large scarf over her head and turned toward Steiner; he kept his eyes focused on her. Kat made signs with her hands as if she was telling an intense story in Italian.

Steiner nodded his head to Kat. "They've gone out the door. We need to follow them."

"Who was Armand with?" Kat asked.

Steiner tilted his head to one side. "I'm sure it was Hanna Winter. She was wearing clothes like yours with an almost identical headscarf."

"You've got to be kidding me. I need to go back upstairs and change."

"We don't have time for that—let's get moving."

"But what if Hanna notices me?"

"Keep your head covered. We only need to see who they are meeting. Remember, even if you try to get the Italians to arrest her for attempting to kill you years ago, we'll never get to know who's behind their trafficking organization."

Kat took a deep breath, wrapped the scarf more

tightly around her head, and followed Steiner out the door. Armand and Hanna were already one hundred meters ahead of them. The air felt brisk as a light drizzle kissed the ground. Small boats floated by on the grand canal with the murmur of Italian boatmen calling out to one another.

Kat slid her arm through Steiner's and walked close to him as if they were partners. If they walked apart, it would be an instant giveaway if Armand and Hanna turned around.

Steiner slowed his steps as their targets approached the entry to the Trattoria Poste VecioVerio Restaurant. "Hanna is going to turn around—kiss me!"

Kat turned to face Steiner. He turned her toward the Grand Canal, embraced her, and locked his lips on hers. A moment later, he released her.

"They've gone into the restaurant."

Kat shook her head to get her bearings. "Damn it Steiner, I wasn't expecting that."

"You want to be walking toward Hanna Winter as she stared at you under a streetlamp?" Steiner asked.

"Good point. I would have had to shoot her. I'm sure she has a gun."

"Where is your gun?"

"In the waistband of my trousers. I'd be happy to do a shoot-out with her."

Steiner laughed. "A kiss is less dangerous, and there are no ricochets."

"You have me there," Kat said. But she didn't say that Steiner had set her heart pounding. For an older man, he was one hell of a kisser.

They entered the restaurant as Kat held back. Steiner held up a menu for Kat. If they couldn't find a table far enough away from Hanna and Armand, Steiner would tell the server they were looking for a different style of cuisine.

Armand and Hanna were already seated at the other side of the restaurant in a corner. A third chair sat empty, waiting.

Kat peaked over Steiner's shoulder. The woman across the room was Hanna Winter. Her blood ran cold in her veins, and she had to force herself to focus.

The server approached, a slim young woman wearing a long white apron, white shirt with black trousers and dark hair piled high on her head. She smiled, offered menus, and told them of the evening specials. Steiner spoke in Italian with the server and pointed at several items on the menu.

Kat listened. She peered over the menu at Hanna Winter. The server walked away, and Steiner leaned forward. "You need to focus on dinner. Our targets are not a floor show."

"Ah, sorry." Kat looked at Steiner and back at her menu. "My apologies. The last time I was in a room with Hanna Winter, she tried to kill me. My gun in my waistband would love to come out so I can shoot her." She shook her head to clear her thoughts. "But you are right; I need to keep up our appearance of a happy couple having dinner. What should we order?"

Steiner smiled. "Never mind, I ordered for us."

Kat put her hand on his. "Thank you. I don't know if I can concentrate to order, let alone eat. Whenever I'm in a situation like this, my stomach is in knots."

Steiner covered Kat's hand with his. "Don't worry, I ordered a few simple dishes with light sauce and a Prosecco. This is the meal I always preferred when I was on missions."

Kat leaned forward, pretending to be enamored with

Steiner, to complete their ruse. "Were those missions' assassinations?"

"Why would you think that?"

"You told me years ago when we first met that you were the number one killer of the East German Communists. I thought you had the highest kill rate in your squad," Kate said, caressing Steiner's cheek.

Steiner smiled. "You do an excellent acting job. I'm sure you have our targets convinced I'm just another lucky old man with a lovely young woman."

"This is Italy. Everyone here has an affair with younger women. I thought it was in the Italian DNA, but you didn't tell me about your kill rate."

Steiner took Kat's hand from his cheek and brushed it with a soft kiss. "I only killed those who—" His eyes focused on the door as a man entered. "We have our visitor."

Chapter Twenty-Three

Kat didn't look up. She kept up the charade of rapture with Steiner and waited until he'd walked past them to Armand and Hanna's table.

"Did you get a look at him?"

The server returned to the table with a bottle of Superiore de Cortizze Prosecco. Steiner tasted it and nodded at Kat. "You'll love this, mellow apples and fresh oranges, and almost yellow, like a true French Champagne."

Kat raised the glass to her lips. "How wonderful." She waited until the server left. "Well, do you know who he is?"

"The number two man in the Romanian mafia. His name is Sorin Lupu. He's done time in the UK for smuggling people into the country and then putting them to work in construction as slaves."

"Well, I guess if you manufactured containers to carry humans, this guy would be the one to fill them," Kat said as she downed her Prosecco. The wine made her stomach relax; she was feeling ready for action. The handgun in her back waistband had a comforting feel to it.

"Seems like they are having a very heated discussion," Steiner said.

"Yes, and I'm wondering why they'd meet here."

Steiner looked at Kat. "Good point. But then again, this is a tourist destination, even in November."

She smiled at Steiner as the first course arrived. He'd ordered an antipasto of sautéed shrimp and calamari with pickled vegetables. She stuck her fork in the calamari and took a bite.

"This is divine," Kat said, rolling her eyes.

"Eat up, our targets are leaving," Steiner said.

Armand and Hanna got up from the table with the Romanian gangster and walked toward the door. Kat turned her head to one side as Hanna walked by. She felt a wind of bodies blow by her. It felt ominous and gave her a chill.

"Do we follow?" Kat asked.

"Absolutely," Steiner said. He threw a wad of euros on the table and guided Kat toward the door. The server watched with slight interest and a smile at the large amount of cash.

They came out of the restaurant to see the three targets heading for the canal. Kat wrapped the scarf around her neck to ward off the cold and hide her face in case their targets turned or stopped.

"Don't you think it's strange they left so early?" Kat said.

"I do not know what they are up to—do you want to follow them or call it a night?"

Kat stood there for a moment. "I want to see where they go to next. They might go to meet the others in their organization."

"You're the boss," Steiner said. "But let's proceed with caution. I don't trust Hanna Winter, and that Romanian is a tough character."

"Tougher than you?"

Steiner chuckled. "Well, let's say he's a lot younger than me."

They followed the targets toward the canal as they did before, arm in arm, making it as if they were continuing a tour of Venice.

"They are getting in a water taxi," Kat said.

Steiner watched them as they stepped into a covered water taxi. He peered around the canal. "There's one close by. I'll call him when they leave."

The water taxi slipped away from the jetty and headed to the Grand Canal.

Steiner let out a loud whistle and waved to the taxi. The water taxi fired up its engines and glided to a stop beside them.

The taxi driver helped Kat in; she stepped into the covered area and turned to speak to Steiner. He wasn't there.

Two men held him on the pier.

"Steiner!" Kat yelled.

Chapter Twenty-Four

The boat pulled away—Kat rushed the captain with her gun drawn. Someone hit her from behind.

Blackness.

Kat woke up on a bed in a large room. She looked up to get her bearings. It looked like an opulent hotel room. A ship's horn sounded outside the balcony door. She threw off the covers of the bed and got up. Her head hurt.

She felt a bump on her head. "Wow, they must have hit me." She muttered to herself. Looking down, she saw she was dressed in a pretty silk night dress with a long side split.

"Whoever dressed me last night has good taste," Kat said. She slipped out of the bed and placed her feet on the floor; something warm and sticky greeted her toes.

She stumbled into the darkness to find a light.

"That's not good," Kat said. A large pool of dried blood had seeped into the Persian rug. "Where the hell did that come from?"

It took only a few steps around the bed to find the body

of Sorin Lupu, the Romanian Gangster, lying face down with a bullet hole in the back of his head. A Glock 17 lay on the floor beside him.

Kat looked around for any signs of her clothes or a phone. There was nothing. She knew the gun on the floor would belong to her.

"Oh my God, this is the perfect setup," Kat said to herself. A loud knock on the door with a policeman's voice announced. "*La polizia, apre la porta!*"

Kat strode to the door and opened it. "*Per favore, vieni.*"

Five officers burst into the room with guns drawn. They lowered their weapons and stared at Kat. She had her hand placed on the door jamb and her feet spread wide.

"Did you want to frisk me, or will you do that at the station?"

The men did a quick inventory of Kat in the scanty lace top. A police officer said, "We came to investigate a disturbance in the hotel."

"What time did you receive the phone call? The man in this room has been dead for some time. Was his blood leaking to the room below?" Kat asked.

An officer wearing the rank of *Sovrintendete Capo* said, "We are arresting you for the suspected murder of this victim."

Kat shrugged her shoulders. "I expected no less. Perhaps you could allow me a hotel bathrobe to exit with?"

The officer grabbed a robe from the bed and placed it over Kat's shoulders. He instructed his officers to guard the room until the crime scene investigation team arrived.

Kat took a deep breath. They put handcuffs on her and led her to the waiting police motorboat. As the boat took off, Kat turned to the officer. "Can you tell me if you found any bodies in the canal last night?"

The officer looked at her with wide eyes. "No, we found no dead bodies. Only the one in your room. Why do you ask?"

Kat smiled. "Oh, just asking for a friend." She sat back and let the cool morning air wash over her.

Chapter Twenty-Five

Kat sat in a jail cell wearing a set of sweatpants and a top given to her by the police. The hotel had demanded their bathrobe back. The pants were too large, but she'd pulled the elastic waist tight and tied it up. Her head hurt from where they'd hit her last night, and she had a strange pain on her right butt cheek.

She hoped Steiner had escaped. To her knowledge, they hadn't shot him but held him so he couldn't help her. The police asked her if she wanted a lawyer. She didn't answer them.

Hanna Winter would want Kat to get a lawyer and be a guest of the Italian legal system that would be drawn out for months, if not years. The gun on the floor beside the victim belonged to Kat. The police had done a gunshot residue test on her hands. There's no doubt it would test positive. She'd seen studies of GSR being transferred from a shooter to another suspect just by rubbing the gun on their hand. Her setup was complete.

It was obvious why it took the police so long to come to the hotel. Hanna wanted time to get away. If they'd killed Kat and Steiner, they would have police on their trail. Now, the police had Katriona Sager, a one-time high-ranking Berlin police detective in their cells who had taken out a known Romanian gangster.

Kat rubbed her shoulders and shook her head. "I should have seen this coming. They were too obvious, and Armand was too easy to follow. All of this was a setup from the day Bernadette Callahan discovered the murder of Eric Chan. Hanna knew she would contact me if Armand came to Venice."

A female police officer came by her cell, looked in, and walked away. Kat looked up at her and waved at her. She hoped a coffee might come her way.

Ten minutes later, a different female officer came to her cell. "You have a visitor. Come with me."

Kat was placed in handcuffs and escorted to a small room. The door opened. Karl Steiner was sitting in the room with a large double espresso for her.

"What! How did you get away?" Kat blurted as she entered the room.

Karl put his finger to his lips for her silence. "I told them I was your lawyer," Steiner said. "Here is my card."

Kat looked at the card. "This looks legitimate. Won't they find out?"

"This is still the morning shift of officers. In an hour from now, the heads of the department will show up. I'll be gone by then."

Kat took the lid off the coffee and sipped. "OMG, this is good. Tell me, how did you escape those men?"

"It wasn't too hard. I waited until they were watching

your boat, ducked behind them and threw them into the canal. Hanna needs to hire better tough guys," Steiner said. He moved his leg and winced. "I sprained my ankle. Seems I'm off my game a bit, but other than that—"

"Can you break me out of here somehow? They have me in for murder. Hanna set me up with the dead Sorin Lupu."

"I heard the police talking about the case in the waiting room. They think they have a slam dunk case. You won't last a week in prison before some pal of Lupu's comes to kill you. But breaking you out of here will come at a price."

Kat coughed. Steiner's words made her inhale her espresso. "What do you mean?"

Steiner put up his hand. "I've already set the wheels in motion. You should get a visit soon from your former police division."

"You contacted my old boss Braun with the BKA?" Kat said with a gasp.

"They are the only ones who can help you. I know for a fact your BKA holds several high-level felons in Berlin that the Italians want."

"But why would my old unit want me back? I quit, remember."

"Yes, you did, and you were the best they ever had. I know Director Braun wants you back in the unit."

"What crazy person told you that?"

"Director Braun."

The door opened; the female police officer looked at Kat with a new respect. "You have a visitor from the German Police."

"That's my cue to leave," Steiner said as he rose with effort. "Now, be nice to her. The Germans are your ticket out of here. They can get your charges dropped and a retraction by the Italian police regarding your crime." He limped out of the room.

"And all I have to do is—"

"Dance with the devil," Director Braun said as she walked into the room.

Chapter Twenty-Six

Director Braun of the German Bundeskriminalamt, the central police agency of Berlin strode into the room wearing her full uniform. Kat knew she'd worn it to impress the Italians. They might not respect Braun, a woman in her late fifties, heavy set with a scowl on her face, but in the uniform —she looked formidable.

"I heard you were in a bit of trouble," Braun said. She dismissed the policewoman with a wave of her hand.

Kat shrugged. "I've been in worse." She leaned to her left to ease the pain in her buttocks.

Braun shook her head. "This is complicated, but I can get you out of this."

"And what do you want?" Kat sighed because she already knew the answer.

"Come back to work for the department. We need you. You were a good detective; you got close to the smugglers, but you let your guard down. The Detective Katriona Sager I knew would have had backup, failsafe plans, and secondary assets in place. You think you are a female 007. It's a delightful fairy tale, but the ending doesn't look good," Braun said as she waved her hand in the room to make her point.

"And if I don't want to work for you?" Kat asked.

Braun tightened her lips and looked around the room. "The Italian justice system works at a snail's pace. I hear you have a lot of money now. But what if they don't let you leave the country?"

"Okay, okay, I'll come back. But only for six months. How is that?"

"You will make it a year. We need you to work on the traffickers in Hamburg, and I heard that is who you've been chasing. You will have more assets if you work with us."

Kat grimaced as a wave of pain shot up from her buttock. "Can you put Stephan back on my team?"

"You almost got him killed twice. Do you think he'll want to work with you?"

"He's good in a fight and smart. I don't want any of the old guard on my team."

Braun laughed. "I love how you talk. In a few seconds, you demand a team and your own young bloods to do your bidding. Okay, you can have Stephan. But you must promise to take care of him."

Kat stood up from the table. She couldn't sit anymore. "Thank you, Director Braun, I promise I will take care of Stephan. How soon can we work together?"

Braun smiled. "He's waiting outside. I knew he'd be the first one you asked for. Now, let's get out of here. And tell me, what's with your *arsch*?"

Kat put her hand on her right buttock. "I'm not sure; maybe I fell on it when they hit me."

"I will have someone to look at it when we land back in Berlin," Braun said as she headed out the door.

Kat paused as she followed Braun. She reached around and felt several bumps on her skin. Heat emanated from the bumps like they had become infected. Shaking her head, she continued out the door.

Chapter Twenty-Seven

Kat welcomed Stephan with a handshake. She longed to embrace him and kiss him on the cheek. However, German and police decorum caused her to maintain eye contact with him and shake his hand while slightly bowing her head. Formality was key with the Germans.

"Good to see you, Kat. Glad to work together again," Stephan said with a slight smile. He was as handsome as she recalled.

Kat had changed into her own clothes with the luggage Steiner brought for her at the Italian police station. They flew back in the private jet used by the BKA special police and arrived in Berlin a few hours later.

Braun had a medical team meet them on the tarmac. She turned to Kat. "Detective Sager, the medics will take you for a complete examination."

"I am fine. I have a headache, but I'll be fine in the morning.

Braun approached her and whispered, "You were

unconscious in the presence of known criminals. The medics will take you to our team of doctors. They will examine you for any foreign substances they might have given you. I've asked them to do a full body scan to ensure they have not injected a tracking device under your skin. Perhaps that is why your buttocks hurt so much."

Kat sighed. There was nothing much she could do. Stephan picked up her bag. "I'm going to be your bodyguard while you're with the doctors. If they spring you early, I'll take you for beer and Döner Kebabs."

"I expect you in my office at 0800 hours," Braun said.

"Am I a BKA officer or a special consultant, Director Braun?" Kat asked.

"You work for me. You decide, but you will treat my office and my officers with the same respect as if you were in the ranks, understood?"

"Ja, Herr Director," Kat said with a salute and got into the medical van with Stephan.

The medics laid Kat on a stretcher and began checking her vital signs. She could do nothing but breathe and let them poke and prod her. Forty-five minutes later, they arrived at a private medical clinic close to the Brandenburg Gate.

A team of nurses surrounded her, changed her into a patient gown, drew blood, and swabbed all her orifices. Then they wheeled her into a room and did a full body scan with an MRI.

Two hours later, a female doctor walked into the examination room. The doctor took her pulse, looked into her eyes, and jotted notes on her iPad.

"Tell me about the tattoo on your buttocks," the doctor asked.

"What tattoo? Don't I have a rash from a fall?" Kat asked.

The doctor shook her head. "You have six numbers tattooed on the bottom of your right buttock. It was not treated with antiseptic, causing it to become infected. I will bandage the tattoo and give you some salve and antibiotics that will clear up the infection."

Kat passed the doctor her cell phone. "Could you take a picture of the tattoo for me, please?"

The doctor took the cell phone and snapped a photo. "Were you drunk when you had this done? It does not appear to be very impressive."

Kat looked at the photo. "It's a series of six numbers. What the hell?"

The doctor shook her head. "Take better care of yourself."

"Thanks for the advice. Am I free to go?"

"Yes," the doctor said. "Our examination reveals no foreign substances, and more importantly, nobody attempted to do anything to you, except for the tattoo."

"That is a great relief, doctor," Kat said.

Kat walked out of the medical office, put her arms around Stephan, and kissed him on the cheek. "We have a mystery to solve."

"What is it?"

"I have a series of numbers tattooed on my right buttock. Hanna Winter was certain that I would overcome the murder charge she tried to implicate me with in Venice. These numbers must correlate to a place."

"Can I see it?"

Kat opened her phone, and Stephan looked at it with interest and chuckled. "I was hoping you'd show me your butt one day, not like this, however."

Kat punched him in the arm. "Let's go for a beer. It's past lunchtime, and I need a kebab."

They found a street-side Döner Kebab with tables on the sidewalk. The sun radiated a comforting heat, creating a sense of tranquility in the air. Kat bought two Berliner Pilsner from the market. They unfolded their Döner Kebabs of beef and lamb and took large bits.

"Aren't you curious about the possible meaning behind the numbers?" Stephan asked.

"Of course, but as a good German detective, I need beer and food first. My mind goes all fuzzy if I don't have food."

Stephan laughed. "Okay, you eat, I'll check your butt numbers."

"Not funny." Kat pushed her phone to him and opened it.

Stephan focused and read the numbers. "Three, five, one, eight, five and one. Did you overhear any conversations in the room?"

Kat took another big bite of her kebab and shook her head. "I was unconscious the whole time."

"The numbers are too high for a combination lock." Stephan sipped his beer and stared at the puzzle. "Wait, it could be a latitude or longitude."

"Do you think Hanna Winter wanted to tell me where my butt is? If you stare at it long enough, you might get some directions."

Stephan put the phone down. "Sorry, I got transfixed with this dimple on your cheek."

"This is not about my dimple—it's the numbers we are trying to solve."

"I'm going to put the numbers in as a latitude and see what happens." He punched the numbers into his phone and looked up at Kat. "It comes up with a soccer stadium on the Ivory Coast in Africa."

"That can't be it; we need something that relates to Hamburg. I'm going to call my detective in Canada," Kat said.

Chapter Twenty-Eight

Bernadette saw the number from Germany come up on her phone. She walked out of the Serious Crimes Division office and took it into the hallway. Several officers walked by her and nodded.

"Hey, Kat, what's up? Did you locate Hanna Winter?" Bernadette asked.

Kat moved away from the table. "Yes, but I got more than I expected." She filled Bernadette in on her previous night.

"Damn, you've been through the ringer! Are you okay?"

"Yeah, I'm fine—and don't worry, I had a complete medical check. The bastards did nothing to me—except tattoo some numbers on my ass. That was Hanna Winter's sick sense of humor."

"Will you send me the numbers?"

"Yes, I will text them to you. We tried to figure out if they were a location, but using them as a latitude, we got a soccer stadium on the Gold Coast in Africa."

Bernadette slapped her hand on the hallway wall.

"Hanna Winter knew I'd call you to follow Armand—she set us up, and we fell for it."

"Same here. She was too easy to follow, and I should have known from the fancy restaurant in plain sight. I've become soft in my old age," Kat said.

"Old age! What are you—thirty?"

"I'm thirty-two. That's almost thirty-five," Kat said in a defensive tone.

Bernadette shook her head. She was twelve e years older than Kat; she didn't want to tell her of the perils that awaited her.

"Yes, you'll need to be more careful at your age," Bernadette said with a grin.

"See what you can find out about the numbers at Paradis Transport, and I'll check here. And please be careful. Hanna Winter could come after you again."

A chill came over Bernadette. "You're right. We live out of town; I'll need to upgrade the security in my place. Thanks for mentioning that."

"I will get you the security company I used the last time I was in Canada?"

"Weren't they ex-East Berlin spies you used?"

"But they were excellent," Kat said.

"Didn't they help you break into a place we had under surveillance and rescue hostages?"

"Yes, they did. I will have them place laser trip wires to ensure no one enters your property without you knowing about it. Their service is my treat, the least I can offer."

Bernadette nodded her head. "Thank you. I intended to use native Indian booby traps, leaving intruders hanging from trees. Your system sounds more sophisticated and humane."

"You are welcome. I will update you on our progress here."

"Oh, one more thing."

"What's that?"

"Don't bother getting your tattoo taken off. They use a laser that hurts like hell. Just have another one put over it. I had a raven tattooed over my gunshot wound. You could do something similar."

Kat looked over at Stephan, he was eating his kebab. "My police partner suggested I tattoo the German eagle over the numbers. But I'm not sure. That's a bit too patriotic for me. I will see when this case ends."

"Good, we will keep in touch," Bernadette said and closed her phone. She walked back into the Serious Crimes Division. Evanston was hovering around her desk, looking for her.

"Ah, there you are," Evanston said. "I got news from the Crown Prosecutor's office. Sanjay Chadha is out on bail, but he's had to surrender his passport, and his lawyer has pressed for a speedy hearing."

"How long have we got?" Bernadette asked.

"A week to ten days, if we're lucky. His lawyer stormed out of the courtroom, muttering about all the motions she would file. And Sanjay is considering recanting his testimony, although he agreed to stay under police protection while he's on bail."

"Once he's back in India, we'll never get him back. Our chance of solving Chan's murder is gone with him," Bernadette said.

"You thinking we have to find Kaitlin Godwin?"

"Yeah, she's our only hope. One of our suspects is lying.

We need to get them together to sort out the truth. Did you find out anything from Godwin's friends and relatives?" Bernadette said.

Evanston pulled out her notepad. "Most were shocked she disappeared. The man she fled with surprised them."

"Why is that?"

Evanston read from her notes. Here's a quote from Kaitlin's best friend of many years: "Kaitlin's new partner blew me away. He just didn't seem her type."

"And what type was that?" Bernadette said.

"According to her best friend, Taylor Pendleton, Kaitlin liked super macho guys and older, rich guys. She said Kaitlin's new partner reminded her of Mitchell Pritchard on the Modern Family television show."

"OMG, please don't have this conversation out of this office," Bernadette said.

"I didn't say it. I just wrote it down. It's common knowledge that our little town is redneck and conservative. How else would you expect them to typecast someone they think is gay? They use stereotypes they see on television. I doubt if they've ever met a gay person," Evanston said.

Bernadette arched one eyebrow. "I bet they have and don't realize it. But let's get down to business. Does anyone know where she went?"

"According to Ms. Taylor Pendleton, the place Kaitlin loved the most is Vancouver Island. She has relatives and a school friend there," Evanston said.

"We need to send uniforms to all those contacts. We have the license plate of her vehicle. Let's run it through all the webcams with the British Columbia ferry service."

"I'm on it," Evanston said. "I'll contact the RCMP near the ferry terminals and on Vancouver Island."

"Good. Give me an update if you come across any

matches. I'm going to visit Sanjay Chadha. I need to find answers to some mysterious numbers. Is he staying at our usual five-star establishment?" Bernadette asked.

"You bet," Evanston replied with a raised eyebrow. "The cheapest hotel we can afford without the bedbugs."

Chapter Twenty-Nine

Kaitlin Godwin parked her jet-black F-150 Platinum crew-cab pickup truck outside the truck stop on the Trans-Canada highway. They'd just driven over the Coquihalla Highway from Kelowna to Hope, British Columbia that was considered treacherous at an elevation of fourteen hundred meters. Driving snow and high winds had pelted the truck for most of the journey. She had handled the road well with her big four-wheel-drive truck, but passing the big transport trucks and dodging other cars swerving in the snow had left her exhausted.

"Are you okay?" Bryson Chandler asked. He was twenty-seven years old, tall, muscular, and handsome, with styled dark hair.

Kaitlin leaned back in her seat. "Yeah, I'm okay. That mountain highway was a nightmare. If I wasn't pregnant, I'd be hitting the bar and doing shots of tequila to calm my nerves."

Bryson unbuckled his seat belt and slid toward her. "It's

important for you and the baby to settle down. Unbuckle your seat belt and let me massage your shoulders."

Kaitlin turned toward Bryson and let his strong fingers work their magic on her shoulders and back. "OMG, Bryson, you are so incredible, and you give the best massages in the world."

Bryson laughed. "What can I say? I have supple fingers and a magic touch."

Kaitlin turned her head, "Is there any way we could turn your gayness off? You'd be such a wonderful lover."

"Sorry, dear, not going to happen. Remember, I'm only on loan to you from Sanjay. I'll be in India with him soon, living down the road from his place with a cadre of my own servants."

"But you understand it won't last, right?" Kaitlin said.

"Oh, and your affair with Armand Paradis is any more real. I chose my fantasies as I see them, but I don't care. Perhaps after Sanjay I'll find someone who looks like Keanu Reeves to live in the Matrix with."

"Oh, Bryson, I've so grown to love you, and I'm going to miss you," Kaitlin said. She turned back to him, holding a gun.

"What are you doing?"

Kaitlin turned the gun around and handed it to Bryson. "We need to part ways. Hanna Winter will look for me once she finds out I'm carrying Armand's child. The police will come to question me regarding Chan's death."

"But what about witness protection?" Bryson asked.

"I don't want my child to grow up being on the run. There's an old friend of mine that I've told few people about on Vancouver Island."

"Is that Amy Nomura, who lives near Duncan?"

"I told you about her?"

"Of course you did. You said I gave you better foot massages, made better sushi and kept a much cleaner house. How could I have forgotten that?"

"You need to forget I ever mentioned her. I want you to take this gun and drop me at the bus depot in the next town. I'll take a bus to the ferry terminal, and Amy will pick me up in Nanaimo on the Island. She has a houseboat on Maple Bay that's out of the way. I should be safe there, but it's you I'm worried about."

"Me? I've played a straight guy to appease your right-wing conservative father, but that's not a crime." Bryson protested.

"You don't understand. Hanna Winter was the one who had Eric Chan murdered two years ago. I'm certain she murdered Armand's two sons over seven years ago."

"Why would she do that? Who would kill two innocent men?"

"I met her when she worked for Paradis Transport. There was an evil in her. Despite her perpetual smile, her eyes held an intense focus on you. It makes me shudder to think about her," Kaitlin said, putting both her hands to her head to block out the image.

She put her hands in her lap and composed herself. "Listen to me, Bryson, after dropping me at the bus depot, please board a plane to India or any safe location. Leave my truck at the airport. That will make everyone think I've left the country and throw them off my trail."

Bryson reached forward and surrounded Kaitlin in a big hug. "Oh, my dear, you've become such a wonderful friend. I thought I might even learn to enjoy watching women's mixed martial arts fighting and eating nachos with you. I'm so sad it had to end this way."

"Stop it, you'll make me cry. Now, take me to the bus depot and get you on your way."

Bryson dropped Kaitlin off at the bus depot, and after tears and hugs, they parted ways. He'd promised her he'd go straight to the airport, but he diverted to the heart of Vancouver to visit old friends in Yale Town. His friends, Yosef and Carrol, lived in an upscale loft near some of the best restaurants in the city. He longed for some authentic Italian food before he flew to India.

He pulled off the main highway and headed toward the center of the city. A white panel van followed him.

Franco sat in the passenger's seat of the van. Gustave, a large man who had been recently released from serving three years in prison for assault with a deadly weapon, gripped the steering wheel with his large hands.

"Don't follow too close. We don't want to scare them," Franco said.

"I don't want to lose them," Gustave said in a voice that sounded like gravel being dumped by a truck.

"Do not worry. I had the GPS locater on their truck activated," Franco said. He smiled as they followed the large vehicle down the highway. Kaitlin Godwin had forgotten that she'd leased her vehicle from Armand Paradis Motors. It was a simple request to the leasing manager to activate the monitor...once he had slammed his head against the wall to remind him who he worked for.

Chapter Thirty

Bernadette Callahan drove to Sanjay's hotel in a shopping area near the highway. Constable Colin Saks stood outside the door to keep him safe, and from making a run for it.

Sanjay opened the door and motioned for her to come in. A hockey game was on television and several containers of food lay on the table with a bottle of beer.

"Are you comfortable?" Bernadette asked.

Sanjay shrugged his shoulders and flopped back on the sofa in front of the television. "My lawyer says she can get my entire testimony thrown out of court and have me on a plane to India in forty-eight hours."

"That's your call. But you could choose justice for Eric and the innocent humans being transported against their will. Or put your trust in Armand's lawyer and hope the people behind the smuggling think you won't talk when you are free."

Sanjay pushed some Kung Pao chicken around in a container and looked at her. "What can I expect my life to be like if I testify?"

"I won't lie. The difference will rely on the individuals we can incarcerate. If we capture the ringleaders, you can resume your previous life."

"And if you don't?"

"You'll be a target. We'll put you in witness protection to keep you safe."

He shook his head. "I don't like my chances."

Bernadette sat in an armchair across from him. "Without going after the culprits, this situation won't improve, but maybe you can make a difference. We found these six numbers in Europe, and we hope you might tell us what they might correlate to."

Sanjay put down his food container and stared at the numbers. "They bear a resemblance to the last six numbers found on a shipping container. A three-letter prefix is required for the company name, with a separate number showing the container's exact location."

"How would we find it?"

"Without the company name, you have nothing. Containers transit globally in millions. With the three-letter prefix, you narrow it down to a company, and the last numbers lets you locate it. There is a seventh number called the 'check digit,' that is used to quickly validate the identity of the container.

"What is the prefix for Paradis Transport?"

"The identifier is PAR, and if you add the six numbers, you run an AI search, but it might take a week."

"Okay, thanks. You've been very helpful. I hope you'll do the right thing and help us with our investigation," Bernadette said.

"Right now, I'm still leaning toward a get-out-of-jail-free card and letting my lawyer spring me. I hope you don't mind, but I'd rather take care of myself," Sanjay said as he turned his head toward the television and avoided her gaze.

Bernadette set her lips in a tight smile. Her phone rang. She listened to the message and put her phone away.

"I have some bad news, Sanjay. The Vancouver police found Kaitlin Godwin's vehicle in downtown Vancouver. Two witnesses claimed seeing two men forcefully remove a young man from a car and throwing him into another vehicle."

"Oh my god, they got my Bryson," Sanjay screamed.

Bernadette put her hand on Sanjay's arm. "Whoever has taken Bryson is trying to get to Kaitlin. Have you any idea where she might have gone?"

Sanjay threw his container at the television. The chicken dish splattered the television screen and obliterated the forward charge of the Montreal Canadiens at the blue line.

"How would I know? I can't believe how stupid I was to let that woman have Bryson to play her games. Now, he's gone. They will kill him!" Sanjay screamed.

Constable Saks opened the door and looked inside. "Everything okay in here?" He asked.

Bernadette nodded her head and tried to get Sanjay to calm down.

"The Vancouver police will put out an all-points bulletin for Bryson. I'll need a picture of him to confirm they took him."

Sanjay pulled his phone out of his pocket and opened it. He turned to Bernadette. "Our friends, Carrol and Yosef just sent me this text. They said Bryson told them he was parking his vehicle and would come right up to their apartment. That was several hours ago. They called in a missing person's report. Does that help you?"

"You need to calm down, Sanjay. Give me his photo,

and I'll send it to the Vancouver Police. I'll make sure they understand the importance of this. Have you any idea about Kaitlin's destination? She will be next on their list."

Sanjay wiped tears from his eyes. "She told Bryson she had a friend on a houseboat on the island. I think it was somewhere near Duncan. I don't remember the name of the place, but it was the name of a tree."

"Like cedar, spruce, fir, or alder?" Bernadette asked.

"I'm not sure. It mattered little to me then."

"How about the name of the friend?"

Sanjay closed his eyes and put a hand to his forehead. "I think she was Asian, like Japanese, yes, it was Japanese. I believe her first name was Amber or something similar."

Bernadette wrote it down, sent a quick text with Bryson's picture to the Vancouver police department, and got up to leave. "I'll inform you immediately once we discover anything regarding Bryson. And I hope you'll stay here."

"I'm not going anywhere until you find Bryson. You want my testimony; you get him back," Sanjay demanded.

"I understand," Bernadette said as she left the room.

"Everything okay with our witness?" Constable Saks asked.

"Sure," Bernadette said. "I'm trying to find a houseboat on Vancouver Island that starts with the name of a tree near Duncan, you ever been in that area?"

"Maple Bay," Saks said.

"Where's that?"

"It's just twenty minutes east of Duncan on Genoa Road. My parents used to rent there for the summer until COVID drove up the prices. It's a nice place with a splendid view of the bay."

"Thanks for the information and the travelogue, Constable. I must get back to the office," Bernadette said.

Chapter Thirty-One

Bernadette dialed Sager on her hands-free car phone as she drove back to police headquarters"You have something for me?" Sager asked when she answered.

"My witness claims the numbers on your butt are like ones on a shipping container. I'm going to ask for a warrant to search the records of Paradise Transport to find out where that container is. Maybe the container is one that's fitted to traffic humans," Bernadette said over her hands-free car phone.

"That's a good possibility. But I'm still pissed that Winter would think it necessary to tattoo the numbers on my ass."

"Has to be a strange joke. We've already had some of her goons trying to intimidate one of our suspects." She filled Sager in on Bryson's kidnapping and the missing Kaitlin who was pregnant with Armand's child.

"You must find Kaitlin—she might have an answer for the numbers. And Hanna will have her killed if she finds out she is carrying Armand's child."

"I put the Vancouver Police on the trail of Bryson, and I'm calling in the RCMP on Vancouver Island to assist. Any information you find would be helpful."

"Yes, I will keep you informed," Sager said as she ended the call.

Kat Sager put her phone on her bedside table and turned to Stephan. "My detective friend in Canada might have found the puzzle to the numbers on my buttocks."

Stephan turned to Kat. They'd spent the past two hours making love and getting reacquainted after their two years apart. He stroked her hair and let his hand fall to her buttocks to massage the tattoo.

"She is quick, but I believe I could uncover something with more examination."

Kat pushed his hand away. "You have done enough examinations. Detective Callahan uncovered a potential connection between the numbers and a shipping container."

"That is why we couldn't find the numbers as a location. The container could be in a port or in transit."

"We will dig deeper in the morning."

Stephan moved closer to Kat. "Well, I could do some digging tonight."

"You've done enough. We need to get some sleep," Kat said with a smile.

"You mean you will let me stay with you tonight?" Stephan asked with a confused expression.

"Of course. The director said you were my bodyguard." She patted his chest. "I must commend you for the good work you've done in keeping me safe. If there was a medal for this, I'm sure the B.K.A. would give it to you."

"I'm so happy that I've met with your satisfaction. If you should need a repeat performance of my duties this evening…"

"*Nein, men schooner mann*. You have done well for tonight. Go to sleep."

Stephan had a broad smile on his face as he cuddled Kat to sleep. She had called him her handsome man in German. How wonderful was that?

He fell into a deep slumber and never heard someone rattle the apartment door. The door, made impregnable by Kat's contractor, stood strong. A sensor would alert her someone had tried to force it open.

Chapter Thirty-Two

Kat Sager poured herself a coffee and looked out the window at a gray Berlin morning sky. Stephan was in the shower, and her regret over last night's events was festering in the back of her mind. She'd never let a man sleep with her after sex; this was a first, which signaled she might be ready for a commitment, but that thought scared her more than Hanna Winter.

She sipped her coffee and tried to push the thoughts away as she picked up her phone. A light flashed on the door sensor app. One tap opened the sensor to show a man had stood at the door at 2 am.

"What the hell! Stephan, you need to see this," Kat yelled as she raced to the bathroom.

Stephan stood wrapped in a towel. "What is it?"

"Someone was at my door last night."

"But they didn't get in—what is the problem?"

"They got by the front door security guard. Get your clothes on, bring your gun, and follow me."

Stephan pulled on his pants, threw on his shirt, and

slipped on his boots in seconds. He checked the ammo of his Glock handgun and followed Kat out the door. They ran down the stairs with guns drawn.

As they burst into the lobby, several tenants looked at them in horror. Kat yelled, "We are police. Clear the lobby."

"Stephan, cover me," Kat commanded. She ran to the concierge desk. It was empty. Stephan came up behind her.

Kat pushed the office door open. The night security guard, Herman Handschuh, lay on the floor, shot in the back of the head.

Two hours later, they met with Director Braun in her office to examine the security camera footage. Braun looked up from her computer screen. "The man at your door was Bogdan Dalca, he is a first lieutenant of Sorin Lupu's gang."

"Do you think Hanna Winter sent him?" Stephan asked.

Braun shrugged her shoulders. "I don't think so. Hanna could have killed Detective Sager in Venice. I believe this was payback for Lupu. As far as his gang is concerned, Sager killed their boss. Winter made certain that once you were out of jail, there would be a team of killers following your every move."

Kat sat across the room, hunched over a fifth cup of coffee. "Ah, my job was getting too easy, and now I will need to be more careful."

"What about the numbers on your buttocks?" Braun asked in her usual dry tone as she tapped keys on her computer.

"My detective in Canada informs me the numbers are

from a shipping container. She has a warrant to check the Paradis Transport Company."

Braun looked up from her computer. "That could be the link."

"How do you mean?" Kat asked. "Link to what?"

"The numbers on your buttocks."

Kat squirmed in her chair. The reference to her butt tattoo was an embarrassment. She sensed Hanna's laughter somewhere in the background.

"You think Hanna Winter wants us to find this container that links to my…ah to my…"

"Yah, to your buttocks. I think the moment we search for the container, you will get a message from her," Braun said.

"Why do you think this?" Stephan said.

"Because it's what any diabolical and psychotic bitch would do. Matter of fact, I must applaud her creative genius," Braun said with a mild grin.

"You are talking about a warped criminal mind," Kat said.

"You are not in a position to remind me of anything, detective. Remember your status. You are a detective—not a freelance crime fighter," Braun said. "I could have you sent back to the Italian jail cell in Venice."

"Ja, mein Direktor," Kat said in German. Her cheeks flushed red with anger. She dropped her eyes to her cell phone.

"Perhaps we should get to our desks to start work on this numbers problem," Stephan suggested. He aimed to calm the room's tension.

"Yes, do that. Let me know what the detective in Canada comes up with it. This may be your link to your backside, detective," Braun said with a wink.

Kat threw a quick salute toward Braun and hurried out of the room. Stephan had to run to catch up with her.

"She pulled her rank on you because you were too informal in there."

Kat whirled to face him. "She's always done that. It's the sign of the supreme power she thinks she has over us because she must eat the crap of her superiors for breakfast."

"It is how the police force works. And Braun got you out of jail to serve with us poor wretches to find clues to human traffickers."

"Damn, you're right. I need to relax," Kat said.

They walked back to a back cubicle and sat beside each other. Stephan turned on his computer and grinned at Kat.

"Are you ready to take on the world again in the old-fashioned police procedural way?" Stephan asked.

"Ja, men Kommandant!" Kat said with a wink.

Chapter Thirty-Three

Bernadette roared down the highway with the police sirens on. Evanston sat beside her, shaking her head. "You don't need the sirens on to do a search warrant."

"The traffic is a pain in the ass, and I need to make it to Paradis Transport before they leave for the day. How do I serve a warrant to an empty building?"

"Okay, you got a point," Evanston said as she looked at her watch. "You got only twenty minutes until they close. Couldn't you get the warrant sooner? My kid has a hockey game tonight."

"I thought your husband covered that?"

"Yeah, it's his darts night, and I told him he could have a night off with the boys. It's how we keep our marriage sane. How is yours doing?"

Bernadette rolled her eyes. "Chris is fantastic. He's taken on the cooking, cleaning, and looking after Raven. Harvey and his partner take care of Raven when we're both at work."

"You paused," Evanston said.

"Yeah…well, I was just gathering my thoughts."

Evanston turned to her. "You don't gather thoughts; you shoot your mouth off like a machine gun with an extra clip. What's the problem?"

"You are a pain—you know that?"

"Ah, and I know when you're having problems. What's going on?"

"I feel like I'm letting them both down. I've been on the job for a week, and I'm hardly home," Bernadette said.

"Sorry, kid. This is the job. You should strive for a work-life balance."

"And have you mastered it, Evanston?" Bernadette said with a narrow stare.

"Not at all. Now, speed up and pass that truck. We have ten minutes before they shut that office down."

Bernadette rolled up on the Paradis Transport building with lights flashing and siren wailing. She jumped out of the patrol car, rushed to the front desk, and produced the warrant.

"I have a warrant to search Paradis Transports for all shipping container records," Bernadette said. She turned to Evanston and said in a whisper, "OMG, I haven't said that in ages. It gave me chills."

The young receptionist looked terrified. She got on the phone to the main office manager. A minute later, a man in his mid-forties, bald and rumpled looking, ran down the stairs to meet them.

"I'm Bertram Smyth, the office manager. What is this?" he demanded.

"Here is our warrant to search all your shipping records.

Please take us to your transport department," Bernadette said.

Smyth looked over the document. Bernadette noticed his hands were shaking. He looked up, adjusted his glasses, and pulled up his trousers. "Very well. I will take you to our transport department and then contact our lawyers."

"Of course. We will need everyone to remain here until we have reviewed your records," Evanston said.

"We don't need everyone here," Bernadette said.

Evanston pulled Bernadette aside. "Smythe is the coach of the opposing team that my son is playing against tonight. If he is here, I have a chance of getting my son to his game tonight. And he's a jerk at the games."

"You are wicked. But I like it," Bernadette said.

Evanston shrugged, smiled, and moved behind the transport manager as he opened his computer.

They spent two hours going over the records. Bernadette stretched, yawned, and looked at her watch. "It's six-thirty. I think we call this a night."

"Yeah, I haven't found one number that would come close. The transport records guy said these records go back several years. I think we've hit a wall."

"What's our next move?" Evanston said.

"I'll call the detective in Berlin and tell her she's going to have to look elsewhere. And I'm going to follow up with the Vancouver Island RCMP. They found an address of Amy Nomura in Maple Bay Marina on a houseboat."

"How do you plan to get Kaitlin back?" Evanston asked as they parked in the police parking lot.

"I'll ask the chief to send me out there to escort her," Bernadette said.

Evanston put her hand on Bernadette's arm. "Okay, you know that thing about work/life balance. It starts when you have a junior constable who could use the overtime to pick her up."

"Yeah, you're right—" Bernadette said as she answered her phone. She listened in silence for a moment. "Yes, I understand. I'll be right there."

"What's up—what's happened?" Evanston said as she watched the color drain from Bernadette's face.

"Chris was in an accident. His truck hit a moose on the highway. I need to go to the hospital."

"Let's get there now," Evanston said.

"But your son's—."

"It's a minor league hockey game, he'll get a ride with a friend. Let's roll."

Chapter Thirty-Four

Kat Sager researched alongside Stephan for several hours. They looked at possible shipping correlations of the numbers she'd discovered in many containers around the world and came up with nothing.

"I read an estimate that there are five hundred million shipping containers in the world, and twelve thousand are at the bottom of the ocean," Stephan said.

"Maybe the number on my bottom is one of those."

"On the bottom of the sea?" Stephan said with a chuckle.

"It's one in the morning. We need to rest. How about if we return in the morning with fresh eyes?"

"Good idea. Do you know what safe house they have us in for tonight?" Stephan asked.

"No, a team of officers will escort us to our new quarters and inform us of the location on the way there."

"I almost feel like royalty—"

Kat put up her hand as her phone rang. She looked at the caller ID. There was none.

"Hallo, Detective Sager."

"Hallo, Sager. Do you recognize me?"

"Hanna Winter. We get to speak at last. Did you want to turn yourself in or give me a long explanation of how your childhood brought you to a life of crime? Was it a hard breakup with a boyfriend?"

"Yes, you are funny, Sager. But it is time I unraveled the mystery of why I did not kill you in the hotel room in Venice."

"I assume it was so the Romanian Mafia would do it for you. That was a lovely setup. But I thought Sorin Lupu was your friend."

"All friends have expiry dates."

"Yes, I can see how you work. Do you have anything to share, or is this just a social call?" Kat said.

"Ah, again, with the jokes. You must find it funny that I tattooed six numbers on your cute little ass."

"I take the cute remark as a compliment. Please continue."

"Here is the punch line. Those six numbers are the key to ten shipping containers somewhere in Hamburg, each one holds fifty women and children. I put a seventy-two-hour timer on the containers as of now. After that time, their air runs out. The numbers are the key. Now. Get off your ass and save them."

The line went dead.

Kat turned to Stephan. "Director Braun was right about one thing. She said the investigation in Canada of the shipping containers might trigger something. It triggered a countdown to the death of five hundred hostages in the containers with the number on my ass as the key to find them before she has them killed. Hanna Winter is loving her evil plan."

"Someone at Paradis Transport in Canada must have called her."

"Yes, or as soon as the Canadian police searched the shipping records, they triggered an alarm back to Hanna Winter. No matter what the sequence, we have lives to save."

"Where do we start? I thought we've exhausted all the possibilities."

"We need to start again. This time, we will investigate the connection Winter had with the Romanian Mafia. She murdered Lupu to set me up. I think that's a way to keep me from finding the container location in their organization."

"You mean because the moment you show your face in Bucharest, they will try to kill you?"

"Yes, that's it. You can see the game she is playing. Braun said she admired Winter's methods as they were diabolical. But I can think like her. We are the same person, but with different wiring," Kat said.

"Thank God for your wiring. I don't think I could make love to someone like Hanna Winter..." Stephan said with a smile that he dropped when Kat frowned at him.

Kat shook her head at his joke and picked up her phone. "I need to call my detective in Canada."

Kat dialed the number. It went to voice mail. She left a detailed message before hanging up. "Let's grab coffee and continue working. We need to pull up everything our organization has on Lupu and his mafia gang."

Chapter Thirty-Five

Bernadette sat in the hospital waiting room with Harvey Mawer. His partner, Ava, was at home with Raven. She glanced only once at her phone and put it down. Time had slowed to a crawl.

How long had they been there? She wasn't sure.

Harvey had appeared at her side hours ago. First, he'd brought her coffee, then water, followed by some indescribable food and more water. She'd eaten and visited the bathroom. All in a sequence punctuated by visits from a female surgeon with lines of exhaustion around her eyes who gave her updates on Chris's condition.

A constable entered the room and walked toward Bernadette.

"Hi, I'm Constable Shana McKendrick. I found your husband on the road, and I wanted to check on how he was doing."

Bernadette looked up at McKendrick. She was all of twenty-two and reminded her of her own first years on highway duty. "Thanks for stopping by. Chris is going to be fine. You arrived in time to save his life."

"He had a severed artery on his leg. When I appeared on the scene, he had duct tape and a belt on the wound. I applied a proper tourniquet from my patrol car. Your husband, despite being fatigued from the blood loss, demonstrated incredible strength."

Bernadette smiled and shook Shana's hand. "Still, you were there. The surgeon said my husband would be okay. There's going to be several months of rebab. It's astonishing how a big moose head can impact a truck cab."

"I've seen worse. A big moose ripped the top off a minivan when I patrolled up north, it killed everyone."

"That must have been terrible to see," Bernadette said as she squeezed her hand.

Shana paused for a moment. "That's what I signed up for. Every accident requires a first responder. I suck it up and do my job."

Bernadette got out of her chair and hugged Shana. "Thanks, constable."

"You're welcome," Shana said. "I understand your husband is an amateur chef. Is that right?"

"Yes, he is. Why?"

Shana looked around to see if anyone else could hear her. "My boyfriend harvested most of that moose with the Fish and Wildlife Department's permission. I'd be happy to bring you a full hindquarter of moose. You know, to see you through while your husband recovers."

Bernadette laughed as tears rolled down her eyes. She hugged Shana harder. "That would be wonderful. We'll celebrate with moose steaks when he gets out of the hospital."

"Sounds good. I wish your husband a speedy recovery. I must return to my duties," Shana said.

Harvey showed up next to her, asking, "What was that about?"

"Long story short, that's the constable who assisted Chris at the crash site—and we got moose meat," Bernadette said.

Harvey shook his head and went back to sitting in his chair. Bernadette took out her phone and checked her messages. She scrolled past one from Chris's mother. That would have to wait until morning. Bernadette had called her the moment she got to the hospital and discovered Chris's condition and given her mother-in-law, Maroula Christakos, updates on his conditions. Maroula, a seventy-year-old Greek widow, considered Bernadette's marriage to her only son an affront to her values. Bernadette was a non-Greek police detective who, in her mind, was responsible for any harm that came his way. Here, the large moose trotting across the highway was somehow Bernadette's fault, and most of that stemmed from her not being Greek.

Her Grandmother Moses left a message, it was simple and to the point. She was on her way from her cabin on the Cree First Nations Reservation in the north to help. That meant the old woman in her eighties had fired up her ancient pick-up truck, packed some wild game jerky (dried meat) and would navigate icy roads for over four hours. She called from Gus's store on the reservation as she had no cell phone. There was no way to reach her to tell her it was too dangerous. Bernadette wiped a tear from her eye. She couldn't wait to see her.

She listened to a voicemail from the Vancouver Island RCMP. They had found the houseboat of Amy Namoura. Kaitlin Godwin had disappeared.

The next voice mail was from Detective Sager in Berlin. She listened to the long message and realized she could do nothing. The world had crashed in on her with a moose on the highway. Moose were dangerous in North America at dawn and dusk when drivers couldn't see them.

The moose that trotted across the highway was looking for its bed for the night. A large truck with headlights would have blinded it. Chris never had time to swerve on the single-lane highway.

She would see what she could do for the other officers in their investigations. But she had an injured husband and a child that needed taking care of. There were two opposing forces about to descend on her home. Grandmother Moses and Grandmother Christakos. Neither would yield, each with differing views on Chris's recovery and Raven's upbringing.

Bernadette shook her head as she headed to see how Chris was doing. She planned to delay informing him about the dueling grandmothers about to descend on their home, as he might want to take on another moose instead.

Chapter Thirty-Six

Braun sat at her desk in police headquarters in Berlin and squinted at the document in front of her. "You think this information is accurate?"

"We discovered it in a file on Lupu from Interpol. They found a long string of transactions between Paradis Transport in Canada and the Romania Mafia shell company in Bucharest," Stephan said.

"The containers are going through Hamburg. It is obvious they plan to use these for contraband," Braun said.

"So much criminal activity gets lost in the shuffle of data. We dug into records from two years ago to locate these files.

"Yah," Braun shook her head. "A low-level analyst sent this to their superior, and it got lost or overshadowed by a bigger criminal activity."

Sager nodded her head. "The police focus on prominent crimes, while small ones slip by unnoticed."

"What's your plan?" Braun asked.

"We head to Bucharest. Lupu has an office in there—"

Braun put up her hand. "You expect to walk into a mafia-run company and ask for documents? Even if you appeared with a warrant, you wouldn't get far."

"We don't plan on a warrant. We plan to get our information at night. They won't know we were there," Stephan said.

"*Ach, mein Gott,* Stephan, you spent too much time with Detective Sager. How will you waltz into Bucharest and break into a mafia office with armed guards and security?"

Kat took a deep breath. She knew the idea might not be well received. "Yes, we know they have security, but Karl Steiner offered us a great team of ..."

"Yah, former East German criminals and spies that I do not want you working with, I forbid you to use them," Braun said.

"Very well. We will ask for help from Romanian Special Forces."

"When are you leaving?" Braun asked.

"In the next hour. We hope you will give us permission for the agency jet."

"Yes, take the jet. I do not want Hanna Winter to murder five hundred women and children in shipping containers in Germany. She will inform the media about the warning we received and use it against us. Our agency has enough bad press. Get out there and do your job," Braun stated.

Kat and Stephan were the only passengers on the agency jet at the private hangar near Brandenburg Airport. After receiving a nod from the captain, they took flight and headed to Bucharest, with a flight time of under two hours.

"Did you mean what you said about contacting the

Romanian Special Forces?" Stephan asked as they left Berlin.

"Not a word of it. If we tried to link up with the Romanians, we would alert Lupu's former friends in the Romanian Mafia. I'm sure they possess contacts with the Bucharest Police. The moment we contact them, we would hand them our lives."

"We are breaking into a mafia stronghold with no backup?"

"No. I contacted Steiner. He has two of the best break-and-enter ex-criminals ready to assist tonight."

"Oh, one of your usual uncomplicated plans," Stephan said. He slumped down in his chair to sleep.

Kat was wide awake. She should have followed Stephan's example to catch a power nap, but her senses were alive. Hanna Winter had controlled the narrative of the events since Venice and everything about this screamed it was a trap.

Kat would enter the lair of Hanna Winter and face off with her. That seemed inevitable from the moment she'd discovered her crimes. One of them would win. Kat liked her chances, but it was not a certainty.

Chapter Thirty-Seven

Kaitlin Godwin had seen the RCMP police cars descend on the little float home village of Maple Bay. She had taken a kayak out that morning to watch the harbor seals and cast for salmon. The sun rose over the hills as the first police car arrived in the village.

Her heart pounded. What could she do? Amy was on her own in her pottery studio. Would they arrest her? Kaitlin sat in the kayak and watched the scene unfold from the shadows of the trees on the opposite shore.

Minutes later, the police took Amy away and placed her in a police car. Kaitlin paddled away as if the situation did not concern her. Two RCMP constables stood on the dock and watched her boat disappear. If they'd used binoculars, they'd have seen a female with the same hair color of the fugitive they were looking for.

Kaitlin rounded the point and was out of their sight in seconds. She breathed a sigh of relief. "What should I do now?" she asked herself.

If the police found Amy's place, they must have Bryson in custody. Her eyes welled up with tears as she realized what she'd put everyone through.

This was from her love affair with Armand Paradise. She rested her paddle and pulled out her cell phone. It was time she set things right.

She dialed Armand.

He answered after several rings. "Who is this?"

"It's Kaitlin."

"Oh, my love. Where are you? I've been filled with so much worry about you."

"You have?"

"I only just heard you are carrying our child. Is this true?"

"Of course, it's true. Who the hell else do you think I've been with?" Kaitlin said.

"Please don't be cross with me, my love. This is wonderful news."

"It is?"

"Of course. I'm so happy for us both. Your pregnancy has given me great joy. I can't wait to see you. I will divorce my wife; I promise this time I will make it happen for us."

Kaitlin broke into tears. "Armand, I was hoping you'd say that."

"But of course, my darling. You mean everything to me. Now, tell me where you are so I can send someone to get you. I'm in Europe right now. But I'll find a little spot for you and keep you safe."

Kaitlin found it hard to speak through her tears. "I'm in Maple Bay on Vancouver Island, but the police are looking for me. They suspect that I am connected to Eric's death. And Armand, I'm afraid of Hanna Winter. If she finds out about us, I'm sure she'll kill me."

"Nonsense. I can control Hanna. Don't you worry about a thing. I will deal with the police. Just give me a minute to locate a safe place for you."

Armand muted his phone and turned to Hanna. "Where should I send her?"

Hanna got on her iPad. "There's a Best Western Hotel nearby. Send her there, and don't let your men screw it up."

"Franco and Gunter have Bryson. They would have picked up Kaitlin had the police not arrived there first," Armand said.

"Why not just shoot her?" Hanna asked.

Armand shook his head. "She is carrying my child. You need to give me this one, Hanna."

"Give you what? Another way to make you vulnerable—"

"—Please, don't be so crass. I did not plan this. But I'm willing to accept her child into my life," Armand said.

"She is your weakness. You need to get rid of her," Hanna said with disgust.

Armand pressed unmute. "Kaitlin, there is a Best Western Hotel as short a distance from you. Can you get to it?"

"Yes, of course. When will you send for me?"

"Franco will pick you up and keep you safe," Armand said.

Kaitlin's hand squeezed the phone with the name of Franco. She'd heard of him. Armand mentioned Franco once when he was drunk, Franco got rid of unpleasant situations.

"Did you hear what I said, my darling?" Armand asked.

Kaitlin blew out a breath and composed herself. "Yes, you said to meet Franco at the Best Western Hotel. I will find it on Google Maps."

"Call me as soon as you get there. I'll contact the hotel and book you in their best room under Paradis Transport. I'll tell them you lost your I.D. while in your boat. That way, the RCMP won't find you. Do you understand me?"

"Of course I do, Armand, my love. I will be there soon."

"I can't wait to see you again," Armand said as he ended the call and dialed Franco. "Kaitlin is heading to a Best Western Hotel near your location. Meet her there."

"Okay, you're the boss, but what should I do with her boyfriend?"

Hanna grabbed the phone. "Franco, kill the boyfriend and Kaitlin. This is Hanna Winter calling. Do you know who I am?"

"Yes, I know who you are…but Armand said…."

"Who are you more afraid of?"

"I will do as you wish, Hanna."

Kaitlin reached the shore and exited the kayak. A sense of despair swept over her. Armand was sending her to Franco. That meant she would be dead. She rubbed her tummy and looked down at her unborn child.

"Mommy has some decisions to make, my little one."

Taking out her phone, she scanned for a taxi or Uber in the vicinity. Neither one answered when she tried to access their apps. Rain pelted down as the wind picked up. Kaitlin pulled her jacket tight and ran through the dense forest.

She followed a trail that took her from the shore to a house near a road. A van passed and then slowed down. She ducked behind a tree. Ominous vibes surrounded the van and the two men.

An hour rolled by before she got up from her hiding

place. She shivered as she ran to a home by the road. There was a Subaru Outback with a kayak on the roof rack parked in the driveway. A light shone in the window.

Kaitlin ran to the door and pounded on the door. "I need your help."

Chapter Thirty-Eight

Bernadette sat beside Chris as he lay in his hospital bed. In a mere twenty-four hours, a lone moose crossing a highway had turned their world upside down.

Chris stirred, raised his hand, and looked at Bernadette. "Hey Bernie, I think I remember getting into a tussle on the highway with a big moose. How am I doing?"

Bernadette stroked his hair and kissed his forehead. "You are fine. The moose's head came through the windshield of the truck and cut your leg. You tied off the severed artery with duct tape and a belt—a police officer was there minutes later with a proper tourniquet."

"I seemed to remember a cute constable coming to me aide. Almost like an angel," Chris winked.

"Yes, she came by to see how you were doing, and Constable McKendrick offered us moose steaks for you to cook up when you get home."

"And that will be when?"

"Real soon, because you're taking up space for sick people," Bernadette said with tears in her eyes.

Chris lifted his hand to place it on her cheek, "Hey, don't we always bounce back?"

"Yeah, we do, but it would be nice if we'd stop scaring each other half to death."

"Well, if we can survive a big moose, we can deal with anything."

Bernadette leaned back and looked at him. "Don't be so sure of that. Your mother flew in from Toronto this morning, and my Grandmother Moses drove in the night before."

"Oh my God. I'd rather take on another moose," Chris said.

"I understand. They told me you'll be returning to outpatient physiotherapy daily for three weeks, then every other day until you can walk on your own."

"They don't think I'll be able to walk?" Chris asked. "Why is that?"

"Your cut was deep. I'm taking you out of here in a wheelchair, and Harvey has built a ramp up our stairs to the house."

"How will I climb the stairs to our bedroom?" Chris asked, looking uncomfortable as reality set in.

"We moved a bed into the library on the main floor. Your mother will be in the guest bedroom beside you, and she will help nurse you back into health."

"She is going to nurse me into insanity," Chris said.

"Your mother meddles in your life because she loves you," Bernadette said with a wink.

"She meddles because she is upset you gave birth to a daughter. And you named her Raven, not my mother's first or middle name. In her mind, you were supposed to give birth to two boys and name them Christos and Nickolas."

Bernadette shook her head and helped Chris to sit up.

"I'm not sorry I didn't meet your mother's expectations. It is our life, not hers."

Her phone rang. She listened for a minute and put it down.

"What's up?" Chris asked.

"A man called the division. He claims he is calling on behalf of Kaitlin Godwin. She wants to come in. But she will only do it if I'm there to protect her."

"You'd better go," Chris said, putting his hand on hers.

"No. I need to put my family first," Bernadette said.

"You need to fix what you started. Harvey can take me home, and you know damn well you don't want to be around my mother while she's fussing over me for the next five hours. Raven will hide with the horses in the barn while my mother creates havoc in our home."

"It's on Vancouver Island. I'll fly there this afternoon and bring her back by this evening," Bernadette said.

"Bring me back a six pack of those great India Pale Ales and some apple ciders," Chris said with a smile.

"This is not a pleasure trip."

"You'll be away from my mother for several hours. Enjoy!" Chris said.

Bernadette went home, picked up a bag, and hugged Raven. "You mind your grandmothers now," she said, brushing her dark hair. Bernadette recognized the look Raven gave her. She would rather hang out with Grandmother Moses than Grandmother Christakos.

Grandmother Moses spoke little to Raven. She let her play and walk into the barn to talk to the animals. When she spoke, she did in riddles, rhymes, and songs. Raven loved her.

Bernadette drove south to the Calgary airport to catch a plane to Victoria. A constable would meet her and drive her to Duncan, a little town forty-five minutes away.

The man who phoned said Kaitlin claimed men were out to kill her. Bernadette had relayed the information to the police in the small town. The man would not give Kaitlin's location until Bernadette landed in Victoria. He said she was terrified of being found by the men trying to kill her.

Franco Marietta waited several hours outside the Best Western Hotel in Duncan. She should have been there by now. He called Armand twice. Both times, Armand had told him to wait.

Franco's phone rang. It was Hanna Winter. "You know she's not coming—find her and kill her."

"We need to go, now," Franco commanded, as he jumped back in the van. Gustave was reading a comic book in the driver's seat and looked at him with annoyance.

"Where? I thought we were waiting for her to come to the hotel."

"She's hiding out back in Maple Bay," Franco said. He pulled out his Glock handgun and checked the magazine, smiled and pulled back the slide to chamber a round.

"You going to kill her?" Gustave asked.

"Yes, and the one in the back," Franco said. "He is starting to stink."

"You ever kill anyone?" Gustave asked.

"Why would I tell you?"

"Because it's different from assault."

"Of course, you think I don't know that?"

"I just got out of jail after a three-year sentence for

aggravated assault. I've never killed anyone, and I don't intend to start," Gustave said, crossing his arms and glaring at Franco.

"Well, your job description just changed," Franco said. He raised the gun and pointed it at Gustave.

"I think you need a little job motivation. You take us to find Kaitlin, and you'll be the one to kill her, or I shoot you right now," Franco said with a grin. "But I'll make you a deal. I'll shoot the one in the back because I think you're fond of him."

Gustave shrugged and started the engine. "I guess I can't argue with that." He stomped his foot on the accelerator. The van lurched forward and picked up speed. Franco hadn't put his seat belt on. He fell toward the door.

Gustave yanked the steering wheel hard right and left, which threw Franco onto the floor. He aimed the van for a lamppost and hit it on the passenger's side. The force of Gustave yanking the steering wheel hard right and left ejected Franco out the window.

The van settled on its side. Gustave pulled himself out of the wreck and opened the back door. He untied Bryson. "You are free to go. If you forget my name, that would be nice, but I don't expect you to."

Bryson staggered down the highway and entered a gas station. Police sirens sounded in the distance as Gustave walked into the forest. He didn't think he'd get far, but he needed some fresh air. He didn't see Franco get up and run across the highway in the opposite direction.

Chapter Thirty-Nine

Two of Steiner's men, Lonel and Avram, who looked in their late twenties with matching muscular builds, picked up Kat and Stephan at Bucharest International Airport. They sat in the back of a black Mercedes sedan and were driven to the J.W. Marriott near the center of the city.

"I didn't know our police force allowed us such nice accommodations," Stephan said.

Kat winked. "They don't. This is on me. I'm tired of the flea traps the BKA puts us in." Especially when the criminals stay in better hotels and often own them. We need a place to keep out of sight. This hotel has great internet, good beds and is within striking distance of our target."

"How do we break into this place?" Stephan asked.

"There is no breaking necessary," Lonel said. "We will be respectable janitors tonight, with mops, brooms and our computer hacking devices." He smiled at them in the rearview mirror and showed off a gold tooth.

"Won't they know we aren't their normal crew?" Stephan asked.

"How often do you notice the janitor in your office, or if you have a new one?" Kat said.

Avram, the younger of the two men with a closely shaved head and a ring in his ear, said, "The mafia gave the office the afternoon off to attend a memorial in honor of Lupu, and we bribed the regular janitors to come in much later." We told them there will be a party at the office to honor their boss. No one asks questions; they only look at the money. There's just one security guard, and he's new."

"Sounds like you have done an excellent recon of the place," Stephan said.

"We learned from Steiner," Lonel said with a wink.

They dropped them at their hotel and drove off.

Stephan turned to Kat. "I am impressed with the talent that Steiner hires. Does he train them?"

"He has a man in Berlin provide an extensive training program that is an offshoot of the original Stasi Police training of the previous German Secret Police of the Communist Block under Russian rule. There are rumors that Steiner's training is superior to anything the Russians had."

They walked into the massive lobby of the J.W. Marriott. The staff directed Kat to the special check-in desk after she flashed her platinum club card. "Two rooms, please."

Stephan stood in stunned silence. Kat handed him his room card and smiled at him. "I need some time on my own, and so do you."

"But…I thought that we'd have a room together for the evening," Stephan protested.

Kat punched the elevator key. The doors opened, and they stepped in. "*Meine Liebe,* you are wonderful in bed and a great lover. I think best alone, and you won't have to worry about the tattoo on my arse!"

"Well, I was going to check to make sure," Stephan said with an embarrassed smile.

"I'm sure you would, and I thank you for your concern." The door opened on the tenth floor. "This is your floor. I am on the club floor. Take a power nap. We will get together soon," Kat said.

Kat took the elevator to the top floor and opened the door to her large executive suite. There were welcome chocolates on the bed, a bottle of Perrier and a half bottle of Taittinger Brut Champagne on ice on the dining room table.

She turned on the taps of the spacious bathtub, poured in some bath salts and undressed into her bathrobe. Her buttock still hurt. The last thing she needed was more of Stephan's attention. A bath accompanied by a glass of champagne would be perfect.

Her toe was about to test the water when her cell phone rang. She recognized it was Steiner.

"How are you?" He asked.

Kat swished the water in the tub and took a sip of her champagne. "I'm good, but I think I'm just springing a trap."

Steiner let out a long, low laugh. "Of course you are. You must figure out how to get the cheese without getting your neck snapped. That is the sign of an intelligent mouse. You, Katriona Sager, must be the better mouse."

"Yes, my friend, I will do my best," Kat said.

"No, do better than your best. Your life will depend on it," Steiner said.

Kat closed her phone and got into the tub. The hot

water and salts sent a sharp pain up her buttocks where the tattoo was. She laid back on the pillow in the tub, sipped the champagne and looked out the window to the Bucharest skyline.

"Okay, Hanna Winter, the cheese is here. Let's see what you've got for me!"

Chapter Forty

Kat woke with a start in the tub. She'd fallen asleep. The water was tepid, and her phone was buzzing.

She grabbed her phone and checked her messages. The Romanian operatives had the cover story in place. The company gangsters were supposed to hold a party there tonight. All employees would be told to leave. Kat and her team had free rein to scan and upload every file that the deceased Lupu and his team had on containers transported from Hamburg.

She felt good. They were on to something, but a nagging feeling in her gut kept telling her that this was a setup. With a quick punch of the keys phone, she dialed Stephan.

"Do you need me to rub your back in the tub?" He asked.

"No, I'm good, thank you." Kat checked her watch. "I overslept. I'll be downstairs in ten minutes."

Kat combed her hair and applied only lip gloss and a mere hint of makeup. She imagined a cleaning woman wouldn't wear too much on her face if she were working. But then she'd seen the makeup women wore in the gym, so she might be wrong.

Lonel and Avram were waiting in the lobby with Stephan when the elevator doors opened.

"It's 6 p.m. We need to get moving; the memorial could end any time they run out of alcohol," Avram said. "They are upset they couldn't get Lupu's body back from Venice because the Italians are taking too long with the coroner's report. Romanian funerals last at least three days with a dead body...in this case, we're not sure what the gangsters will do."

"Could they come back to the office?" Kat asked.

"That is possible," Avram replied. "There's a room in the back where they hold meetings to discuss all the money they've made from the poor souls they have trafficked."

"The police have known of this gang for years, but there are too many bribes to government officials and police to take them down," Avram said.

"It's possible that tonight we can locate something to aid the police." Lonel and Avram looked at each other and rolled their eyes. It was obvious they thought they wouldn't achieve much.

"Sure, let's see what we find," Lonel said.

They walked outside to a large Renault panel van and got into the back. Kat and Stephan found their janitor uniforms and changed into them.

"You could look away while I'm getting dressed," Kat said to Stephan.

"Are you kidding me?" Stephan laughed. "You stared at me when I dropped my trousers."

"I was only admiring your abs," Kat said with a wink.

"Same here."

They rode to the building in silence. Kat realized her stomach was rumbling. Dinner was forgotten in her need to get some rest, and it would be a long time before they saw food. It was the way of chasing criminals. Food and sleep had to be grabbed when one could, and they didn't always coincide with criminal behavior.

Lonel and Avram changed into janitor uniforms when Kat and Stephan stepped out of the van. "Here are your fake IDs," Lonel said.

Kat looked at the fakes. "I'm Aisha Bakir and Stephan is Habil Ahmed. What nationality are we supposed to be?"

"You are Syrian. There are lots of them here. Just respond in English that you are Syrian and don't speak Romanian."

Kat shrugged her shoulders. "I guess that works. Let's get to work."

They signed in with the security guard at the front desk, flashed their fake IDs, and took the elevator to the fourth floor. Avram opened the office door and switched on the lights.

"We must hurry in case anyone comes in," Lonel said. "I will check the main servers and download whatever I find on their shipping containers. Avram will take you to Lupu's old office and search his computer."

Stephan followed Kat and Lonel into Lupu's office. A large mahogany desk occupied most of the room to show the former gangster's prominence, with two leather armchairs for visitors. Behind the desk were pictures of his family on a credenza inlaid with bright brass.

"Nothing says gangster like an overstated office," Stephan said.

Avram opened the computer on Lupu's desk as Kat investigated the desk drawers. She moved on to the credenza and checked out the pictures and mementos on display. There was a picture of an elderly woman who could be his mother and several elaborate carnival masks that looked like ones she'd seen from Venice.

"I see little in his files," Avram said. "There's one file I can't open. It's named Martedi Grasso. And I see Lupu sent it to his laptop."

"Any idea what that could refer to?" Kat asked.

Stephan raised his head from the computer screen. "That is Latin for Fat Tuesday, or Mardi Grai."

"What significance would it be to Lupu?" Kat asked. "Wait, what's that noise outside?"

A loud bang sounded in the front office, and several voices sounded. Avram stuck his head outside the door. "Two men entered the office. Get busy—make like you are working."

Chapter Forty-One

Kat hurried into the main office, picked up the wastebaskets, and emptied them into a large plastic bag. Stephan followed her with a duster and got busy on the desks. They avoided eye contact with the men.

The men were tall, with well-built bodies covered in cheap suits and gold chains around their necks. The taller man with a tattoo on his neck swaggered into the room, speaking to his buddy in Romanian.

Lonel came beside Kat and whispered to her, "They heard rumors there was another party here tonight. I will speak to them."

Lonel spoke to the first man. At first, he waved him off, then he came up to him and stuck his finger in his chest.

Avram came up behind Kat. "The man says he came for a party. He wants to know where it is."

Kat whispered back, "How did he hear that?"

"The other cleaners told him," Avram said.

"They look and sound drunk. They've come from the funeral," Kat said.

"I agree. We must do something."

The big man in front of Lonel noticed Kat. He came toward her, making dance moves, and spoke to her in Romanian.

Kat put up her hands. "I don't speak Romani, only English and Arabic. I am Syrian."

The man put his enormous hands-on Kat's hips and swayed. "We party. Yes!"

"No party," Kat replied as she took his hands away.

The man moved his hands to Kat's throat. His eyes narrowed; his lips tightened. "We party. Yes."

Kat smiled at him. She turned to Avram and spoke in German. "Two moves and he's finished. Can you get the other one, Stephan?"

"Copy that. The other one is already making eyes at me," Stephan said.

Kat moved in close to the man and smiled. "Yes, we party."

The man put both his hands on her waist. She stomped on his foot, grabbed his collar, turned and dropped to one knee, throwing him over her shoulder. He landed with a thud. She descended on his throat with her elbow.

The big man let out a gurgle. Seconds later, the man in front of Stephan was on the floor and unconscious.

Stephan smiled at Kat. "Looks like we must clean up more trash; janitorial work is hard."

"We need to get out of here. The other janitors can't see these two men like this," Avram said.

"You're right. We need to stage them properly," Kat said.

"What do you mean?" Lonel asked.

"Let's put them in Lupu's old office," Kat said.

The men were heavy and took them all of them to drag their bulk into the office.

"But the janitors will find them right away. What good will this do?" Avram asked.

"Remove their clothing and use these handcuffs to position them facing each other. You can leave their shorts on," Kat said.

Avram chuckled. "Ah, the janitors will not know what to do with that." He pulled off the biggest man's pants. "Oh, he is wearing ladies' underwear. Now, we know the other janitors will not want to touch this."

"What if we take a picture to post on Instagram and call it Gangster Love!" Stephan said.

"Let's not push our luck, Stephan," Kat said. "I'm going to take pictures of these masks and the makers' signatures and trademarks before we leave. Hanna Winter murdered Lupu in Venice, and he has ties there. Maybe we have a clue."

Avram looked out the window of the office building. "I see some cars arriving. We need to leave in case more gangsters think there is a party here."

They walked out of the office and took the stairs down to the lobby. They saw four men in suits enter the elevator.

"My oh my, they are going to have some stories to tell," Lonel said.

Chapter Forty-Two

They entered the panel van and changed their clothes. Avram dropped them off at their hotel and left them with the USB stick.

"Let's go to my room to review files and order room service," Kat said.

"I was hoping you would say that."

"You will sleep in your own bed tonight."

"And I was hoping you wouldn't say that."

Kat quickly showered and joined Stephan back at the dining table, wearing her plush hotel robe.

Stephan took a sip of water, looked at Kat, and sighed. She was all business; he got the message. Room service arrived, and they savored the food while sipping on the red wine.

"There has to be some connection to the masks and Lupu," Kat said.

Stephan swallowed the last of his cabbage roll. "Why do you think that?"

"He was a gangster. The only other thing on the

credenza was his mother's picture. Can you find her address?"

Stephan tapped the keys on his laptop. "I found her name in our data files but no address in Venice. Looks like Lupu hid her deep inside the old city."

"I'm sure Lupu left an important file on his computer with his mother in Venice."

"How do you find someone hidden by a mobster? Especially a mobster's mother?"

"I think the masks are a key," Kat said. She opened her phone and scrolled the pictures of the masks from Lupu's office. "They appear to be made by the same artist."

"Let me check the best makers in Venice," Stephan said as he clicked on his laptop. He pulled up several files and compared the masks. "Many of the real artisan shops are in San Palo; the rest seem to be cheap knockoffs."

"What about all those masks you see in the window on the streets?" Kat asked.

"They come from China or anywhere in between. My source on Google suggests that the price of authentic masks is often two hundred euros, beyond what the local tourists want to pay."

Kat adjusted her bathrobe and looked over the translated files Avram had taken from the office. "I see numerous emails between Lupu and his mother. He also claims she shouldn't buy another mask from La Bottega dei Mascareri, as she has too many."

"That maker is on Calle de Saoneri in San Polo."

"Great, but I wonder why they named the file Fat Tuesday," Kat asked.

Stephan shrugged his shoulders. "Maybe the artisans on that street make the masks for the Mardi Gras carnival of Venice."

"I hate it when you come up with such simple answers. We have an idea where his mother shops for masks. Now, I must find out if Lupu left his laptop in Venice. I'm going to access our bureau files on Lupu to see what surveillance we have on him."

"Do you think our department tracked him?" Stephan asked.

"The BKA tracks everyone of interest," Kat replied. She pulled up the recent CTV photos of Lupu. "Here's a photo of him arriving at the Marco Polo airport with a carrier bag that looks like it would hold his laptop. There's no report of them finding one in the hotel room near his dead body. The laptop must be in Venice."

"Are we heading back there?" Stephan asked.

"Yes, I am sure our shipping containers are on Lupu's laptop in Venice," Kat said.

"Why do you think that?"

"Because Hanna Winter wants a showdown with me there. She thought Lupu's men might kill us, and it didn't happen, and the trail from Lupu's office back to Venice is too obvious."

"I'll call Avram and Lonel and tell them to pick us up for our trip back to the airport," Stephan said.

"Great, I will send a message to Director Braun and request backup sent from Berlin and clear me with the Italian authorities, just in case they have a file of my arrest open."

Stephan glanced down at his phone. "Avram is not answering."

Kat ran to the window. "Their van is still in the parking lot—there's no sign of Avram or Lonel. And I see two cars with four men close by."

"Do you think the Romanian gangsters killed Avram and Lonel?" Stephan asked.

"Looks like someone saw us come here. This was an error on my part."

Stephan removed his Glock handgun and chambered a round. Kat threw off her bathrobe, jumped into her clothes, and pulled out her gun. She went to the window and looked out again from behind the curtains.

"Why haven't they moved on us?"

"They might wait for word from their captain. Those guys don't move without commands. We need to get out of here."

A knock sounded on the hotel room door. Stephan went toward the door with his gun drawn.

"Careful. There is a chance they organized a hit team."

Stephan peered through the peephole. "It's Avram."

Chapter Forty-Three

Stephan swung the door open. Avram burst inside and quickly closed the door.

Kat put her hand on his shoulder. "We thought you were dead."

"So did we," Avram said as he tried to control his breathing. "We saw two cars full of men pass us. They were the same ones we saw entering the gangster's office. Lonel followed them at a distance as they entered the hotel parking lot. We thought they might rush the hotel, but I'm sure that would piss off every politician in town if they killed you in an upscale tourist location."

Stephan nodded. "Even the gangsters know that's bad for business. But why didn't you call us?"

"Lonel was paranoid that they might have a cell phone monitor. We found a way out of the hotel that they will never notice."

"Are we going to be janitors again?" Kat asked.

"No, you are going out with the laundry service; the

driver leaves in ten minutes. We've bribed him to take you to your plane."

"Great, nothing says high class like leaving a five-star establishment with dirty linen. I can't wait to write a review," Kat said.

"Grab your belongings. There is no time to waste. Don't use your phones until you are airborne. I used the hotel's land-line to let your plane's captain know you'll be there in an hour."

"But it didn't take that long to reach here when we arrived."

"The linen driver must make it look like he's still doing pickups. We don't want them to follow you to ambush you along the way."

"Your logic stinks—literally," Kat said. She ran to her bedroom, grabbed her bag, and they did the same for Stephan. Minutes later, they were lying on the floor of the linen van, hidden by laundry bags.

The one hour seemed forever as the vehicle lumbered through the streets of Bucharest and stopped at another hotel and two restaurants. By the time they reached the airport, they had stunk of tomato sauce and spices.

The captain greeted them and protected her nose with her hand as they walked onto the plane.

"We need to go to Venice," Kat commanded.

The captain was a tall woman named Linn Fischer, with reddish hair tied into a tight ponytail. She smiled at Kat and looked at her phone. "I'm sorry, Detective Sager, but they directed me to fly you to Berlin."

"Who gave you such an order?"

"Director Braun called me. I am under her command. She will meet you on arrival when we land," Captain Fisher said.

Kat walked back into the cabin and plopped into the chair across from Stephan, saying, "We have been summoned to Berlin."

Kat sat in her seat as the jet reached flying altitude, then pulled out her phone and dialed Steiner.

"What's up? I heard things did not go as planned in Bucharest," Steiner said.

"You could say we stunk up the mission."

"How can I help you?"

"Braun has recalled us to Berlin. But I'm sure we would find the key to the shipping container on Lupu's laptop in Venice."

"And Director Braun thinks you are on a wild goose chase, I take it?"

"Yes, she is meeting us at the airport. I'm sure we will be sent to Hamburg to search for the shipping containers."

"And you need some insights into the workings of Venice and finding hidden gangsters' mothers and laptops to do your own search. Is that correct?"

"Yes, but the numbers Hanna Winter left me are more than to shipping containers. They might solve the riddle of where to find the key to shut off the countdown that could be on Lupu's laptop. My instincts are sending me looking for a mask shop where his mother shopped. If I can find her, I can find the laptop."

"And you think I can find it for you?"

"You are as sharp as ever, even on one foot."

"I will call Enzo in Venice. Text me the numbers you found on your lovely bottom, and I will call you back."

Thirty minutes later, Kat's cell phone buzzed with a call from Steiner. "I checked with Enzo. He gave me a complete run down on how addresses work in Venice. They have only four numbers, you have six."

"So, Venice is a dead end?"

"No, that's the best part. The last four numbers, one eight five one, is the address of a café in San Polo near the Rio Alto Bridge. I think you need to find other numbers that will work with the prime six numbers you have. Hanna is using them as a key for you to hunt for the laptop."

"Oh my god, she is such a bitch."

"But a crafty one. How would you like to travel to Venice?"

Kat looked around the cabin. The captain and co-pilot were busy with the Berlin control tower for their landing, and Stephan was napping. "I will agree to everything Braun suggests, then slip away. How soon can you get me a plane?"

"With your money, the possibilities are endless. I will text you with your flight information in an hour."

Chapter Forty-Four

Kat and Stephan walked onto the tarmac of the private jet hangar to see Director Braun pulling up in a black BMW sedan. She stepped out and marched toward them.

"She looks all business," Stephan muttered to Kat.

Director Braun stopped a meter from them and sniffed. "You reek of garbage."

Stephan and Kat stood at attention; explaining their smell would only make things worse.

Braun paused and let her eyes run up and down both and shook her head. "You have had enough foolish adventures and will resume your regular police duties. I'm assigning you to the task force at the Hamburg docks—report to headquarters at 0700 hours to be transported there. Do you understand?"

"Yes, my director, but how will we find the hidden shipping containers?" Kat blurted and regretted it as soon as she said it.

The director's eyes snapped open. "We will use technology. Something you lack in your constant racing around the country at the B.K.A.'s expense. Our tech department has developed an AI program that has run a complete diagnostic of the numbers on your backside, Detective Sager."

"And they have located the containers we are looking for?" Sager inquired.

"No, but they will by the morning. Enough with the questions. Get out of here and take a shower," Braun whirled, marched to her car and was gone in seconds.

"I guess we have our orders," Stephan said.

Kat turned to Stephan. "Do you believe an artificial intelligence program is going to find ten sea containers in the thousands on the dock in Hamburg?"

"No, I don't, but we've been given a direct order."

Kat grinned. "Only if we follow them." She took out her phone to order an Uber Taxi.

"But I might get suspended from the force, and Braun might send you back to stand trial in Italy."

"Indeed, she could do that, but if we find Lupu's laptop and stop the countdown, we save innocent people."

Looking up into the night sky, Stephan whispered, "Yes, but..."

"Our Uber is here. Are you coming with me?"

"Where are we going?"

"A private jet is arriving at 0700 hours to take us to Venice. I found us a hotel room near the airport. Once we shower and change, we can get back to the Winter puzzle."

Stephan got into the back of the Uber with Kat. "Maybe we can have a quick shower together."

"Do not get your hopes up *mein Schatz*. The only thing I want from you tonight is your attention as we search for clues. And none of them involve us getting closer than your computer."

They checked into the hotel, took separate showers, and

changed. Kat ordered some food from room service, and Stephan opened his computer.

"What are we looking for?" Stephan asked.

"Check anything on Google Maps in Venice that is near the café," Kat said, "I'm going to call the detective in Canada." She checked her watch. It was midnight, which meant four in the afternoon in Canada. Kat dialed the number for Callahan and hoped she could reach her.

Chapter Forty-Five

Detective Bernadette Callahan drove into Duncan to see two police cars, an ambulance, and a fire truck at the scene of a wrecked van. The constable driving pulled up beside the lead patrol car to check on the accident.

"What's the situation?" Bernadette asked the officer.

"The van hit a light pole, and a guy got out and released someone from the back who wandered over to the gas station and told them he was a hostage," the policeman said.

"Did he give a name?" Bernadette asked.

"Yeah, said his name was Bryson Chandler."

"Where is he now?" Bernadette asked.

The constable pointed in the ambulance's direction.

Bryson was lying on a stretcher as a medic attended to him as Bernadette approached. "What became of the men who kidnapped you?"

Bryson shook his head. "A guy named Franco, a super badass that wanted to kill me, got thrown from the van. I didn't see what happened to him. The other guy, Gustave, freed me and ran off into the woods."

"We must find Kaitlin. There's a killer on the loose," Bernadette said to the police officer with her. She dialed the number of the man who claimed he was keeping Kaitlin safe.

"Hello," the man answered.

"This is Detective Bernadette Callahan of the RCMP in Red Deer. The man who held her friend captive is at large. I want her location now. I need to get her to safety. Do you understand me?"

"Just a minute," he said.

Kaitlin came on the line. "Where is Bryson?"

"He is safe, but a guy named Franco is still at large, and so is Gustave. You are in danger. Let us bring you in now!"

The man came on the line. "We are the yellow house on Shore Pine Close. You can't miss it. I'm getting out my shotgun, and if anyone other than a police officer come to my door, I'll blow the bastard away."

"We'll be there in five minutes. Stay calm," Bernadette said.

Bernadette rolled up on the yellow house with two patrol cars as backup. She asked them to cover the area. If anyone tried to approach from the woods, she told the constables to shoot them.

The door opened; an older man stood at the door with a shotgun at his side. He lowered it when Bernadette flashed her badge.

"Sorry for the welcome. I didn't want to take any chances with the young lady. She's scared out of her wits."

Kaitlin rushed out of the house and fell into

Bernadette's arms. "Armand Paradis told me he was sending Franco to get me. He only sends him to get rid of people. I'm so sorry I caused all this."

Bernadette guided her to the patrol car. "It's okay. You're with me now. We'll get you into police protection, and you will be safe."

Kaitlin raised her head. "I'll never be safe while Hanna Winter is alive. She wants to kill me for having an affair with Armand and getting pregnant. I know I have a son; I had the sonogram. But I know now that he wants me dead."

Bernadette put Kaitlin into the back of the patrol car and was about to get into the front when she noticed her phone ringing. Kat Sager was calling.

"I can't talk for long," Bernadette said when she answered the phone. "I have to take a witness into police protection."

"Can I ask who you have?"

"Kaitlin Godwin," Bernadette replied. She was breaching police protocol, but Kat was in Europe and would need the witnesses brought in to solve the human trafficking case.

"How soon can you get her into an interview?"

"Not for a few hours. Why?"

"I'm sure the shipping container's location is on a laptop in Venice. I need to find it, and the clues are in four digits."

"How could I help with that?"

"Hanna Winter is a psychopath and believes she is diabolical. There must be a clue to Lupu's mother's address in Venice with one of your suspects."

"What kind of clue?"

"All the house numbers in Venice have a unique four-digit number, and we need to unravel the secret code to find Lupu's mother's place.

"From the numbers on your butt?"

"Yes, of course, those numbers had four that related to a café in Venice. If we unlock another four, it will give us the address of Lupu's laptop and a way to stop the countdown on the containers with the hostages."

"And the numbers tattooed on your butt correlate to one address to give you a clue? Let me check with Kaitlin right now to see if she knows something," Bernadette said.

A moment later, Bernadette came back on the phone. "The only number Kaitlin said we might want is the four-number access code she used to meet with Armand Paradis at the apartment. She doesn't remember it. It's in a safety deposit box in Red Deer."

"Can you get me the number as soon as you land?"

"Sure, but this is Canada, not Europe. We have a layover in Vancouver before our flight to Calgary and over an hour's drive back."

"Anything you can get me will be appreciated. We have only one part of the puzzle, and Hanna Winter wants us to work for the answer. There are only twelve hours until a shipping container full of women and children runs out of air."

Chapter Forty-Six

Enzo met them at the airport at 0840 hours and took them by water taxi directly to a dock near the Rialto Bridge in the district of San Polo. From there, Enzo guided them along the streets that were deserted of tourists.

"You must tell me something about the person you are looking for. I must know if they have money and if they don't want to be found," Enzo said as they navigated their way over the cobblestones.

Kat looked at Enzo. This man was more than a driver. "She is the mother of a Lupu, the gangster. I doubt her former son wanted her found."

"No, she will not be easy to find. First, she will be on the second or third floor. Locals with money live on the higher floors to avoid the bugs and to keep cool if they don't have air conditioning."

"And what's the second thing?" Kat asked.

"I doubt your lady will be on any busy street near a mask shop. We must look for small streets with only four to ten buildings. The apartments are cheaper, which I think would be what a gangster would buy and out of the way of tourist traffic."

"Do you think the owners of the mask shops might tell us if one of their best customers lives near them?" Stephan asked.

Enzo shook his head. "You are German, which puts you in a negative light for Italians unless you are buying something. If you arrived with the Italian police with an active investigation, you might have a chance."

"So, you are saying we must somehow track this lady down by instinct?" Kat said.

"Yes, and if you had an address, that would be nice, but even then, we would have a problem?"

"Why is that?" Stephan asked.

Enzo turned and with a wave of his hands, began a lecture. "There are six districts known as 'sestiere,' and in each one, there is only one address. No matter the street, there is one number in San Polo for that address or any other district."

"You're saying if we have an apartment number, we can find the person?" Kat asked.

"Yes, if we can find the apartment number, and we are sure Lupu's mother is in this sestiere district, we can locate her."

Kat shook her head. "I take it that Venetians know how to find each other?"

Enzo smiled. "They invented the system, and it works for them. We must be careful as we wander the streets looking for this lady. I have brought along cameras for you to look like tourists. If we are too obvious, we might set off an alarm amongst the residents, and the police will come to ask us questions. And, if Lupu has left a person to watch over his mother…"

Kat looked at him. "Our lives are in danger. Is that what you want to say—"

"That is, it."

"Thanks for your warning, Enzo. I hope I might have a number in a few hours," Kat said as she looked at her cell phone. It had buzzed with text messages several times. Director Braun had sent several texts, each becoming more threatening and demanding. The sergeant of the Hamburg task force had noted Stephan and Kat's absence. Braun warned, *'If you are in Venice, against my orders, I will have the Italians throw you both in jail.'*

Chapter Forty-Seven

Bernadette Callahan experienced a delay in her flight to Vancouver. But they made their connecting flight to Calgary by running the length of the arrivals concours for the one hour and twenty-five-minute flight to Calgary.

Kaitlin's nerves were on edge, and she couldn't sit still during the entire journey. Bernadette had to whisper to her and keep her calm. At one point, Kaitlin almost exploded. Bernadette held her hands and whispered to her, "Right now, I need to get you back to Red Deer. We will keep you safe, but first, we need to get a code from your mother's house."

"I just want to put my feet up and rest. I've been under too much stress," Kaitlin said.

Bernadette took both her hands and stared into her eyes. "I need you to help me solve a case that involves the safety of hundreds of innocent women and children. Hanna Winter has threatened to kill them if we don't find them. A detective in Europe thinks a code you have in your safe deposit box might be the answer. Are you willing to help?"

Kaitlin wiped her eyes and sniffled. "Oh God, I'm totally willing to help. Why didn't you mention this sooner? We need to get moving. My bank closes at 5!"

The plane landed at 3 pm. Kaitlin rushed through the terminal after being the first off, the plane. The young pregnant woman's speed surprised Bernadette.

By 3:15, they hit the highway north. Bernadette put her lights on and hit the gas. They made it to the outskirts of the small City of Red Deer at 4:15.

"Oh crap!" Kaitlin screamed.

"What is it?"

"My key to the bank deposit box. Bryson has one, and my mother has the other."

"Where is your mother's house?"

"She's away on a two-week cruise."

"Do you have a key to her house or know the neighbor who has one?"

"I don't have a key, and the neighbor hates me. Her son was a scumbag, and I wouldn't date him."

"You are making things difficult," Bernadette said as she hit the hands-free on her cell phone.

Evanston answered, "Hey Bernie, you back in town?"

"Yeah, and I need a uniform at the address of Kaitlin Godwin's mother. There's about to be a break-in."

"Do you see it in progress?"

"No, I'm going to do it. Have a uniform standing by. We need an important piece of evidence at the house."

"So much fun when you're around. I'll make it happen," Evanston said.

They rolled up on the house with the car's light flashing. Bernadette got out of the car and walked to the neighbor's home and knocked on the door. There was no answer.

She walked back to Kaitlin's mother's house and kicked the door in just as the patrol car arrived.

"What's going on?" the constable asked as he walked to the house.

"I had to break into this home to secure a safe deposit box key that is vital in the case I'm working on," Bernadette said.

"Are you going to fill out the paperwork?" the constable asked.

"Yes, I will just need your badge number for reference and the insurance claim for the homeowner."

"Works for me."

Kaitlin pulled her head out of the car. "I'll make sure one of our friends boards up the door later."

The constable smiled. "No problem. You have a nice evening."

Kaitlin ran into the house, opened a cupboard door in the kitchen, and pulled out the key. "We've got fifteen minutes."

Bernadette put on her siren and hit the gas. Five minutes later, they were in front of the bank. She ran in, flashed her badge, and asked for the manager. The woman looked frightened until she recognized Bernadette.

"What's going on?" the manager asked.

"We need to get a safe deposit box open," Bernadette said.

"Sure, not a problem. And there's no rush. We're open until eight."

Bernadette shook her head as Kaitlin walked to the back of the bank. "You think you could have checked their website?"

"I've got it," Kaitlin said as she walked back with a small piece of paper in her hand.

Bernadette texted the number on the paper to Kat Sager.

Chapter Forty-Eight

Kat's phone buzzed with a text. She shook her head as she read it. "Hanna Winter is true to form. The number that Kaitlin Godwin had is one eight five one. That's the same number of the last four numbers of the shipping container we are searching for."

Stephan scratched his head. "What were the four numbers for?"

Kat read the text. "The Canadian detective states these four numbers were a code this woman used to enter an apartment to meet Armand Paradis in secret."

Stephan chuckled. "It wasn't a secret to Hanna Winter. She made it part of the shipping container."

"And we assume it's the address for Lupu's mother's place. Which seems impossible if it's right," Kat said.

"Why is it impossible?"

"Hanna Winter would have had to know the exact address of Lupu's mother and have the code a woman in Canada was using for an affair with her lover." She turned to Enzo and showed him the numbers.

He did a Google Maps search on his phone. "I'm afraid you have the same number as the mask shop on Calle dei Saoneri in San Polo. Perhaps the woman is playing with you?"

"Yes, she is playing with me. If the numbers on my butt match something in Canada, then indeed, this a big game —to her! Kat said.

Kat texted back to Bernadette. "Do you have any other codes from anyone else? The address was the same as the mask shop."

"The mask shop is open now. I suggest Enzo tell the owner he's looking for his lost aunt," Stephan said.

"What, an Italian man looking for a lost aunt from Romania?" Kat asked. "I can't see how that will fly. We'll have every Polizia Di Stato here in fifteen minutes and waste valuable time explaining ourselves."

Stephan shrugged his shoulders, and Enzo stared at the sky. The sun was breaking through the clouds as a light rain fell, and a rainbow formed an arc over the Basilica of St. Mark.

"Then we must find a place for a morning cappuccino and cornetto. I think you call it a croissant, but the Italian version is sweeter, while the croissant is a dull cousin, as we say in Venice," Enzo said with a wave of his hand that dismissed many years of French culinary history.

"We can do that later, Enzo. I will be the cousin of Lupu's mother as Stephan suggested. You will translate for me, and we will attempt to find her," Kat said.

Enzo shook his head. "So, that is no to the coffee and cornetto?"

"Yes, later. Let's go into the mask shop," Kat said as she pushed Enzo forward. "Tell him I'm looking for my cousin and I only had the address of the shop. My cousin told me that she lived close by. Show him the picture of Lupu's mother on my phone."

Enzo moved slowly as Kat followed him to the door. He entered the shop and engaged in a long conversation with the shop owner, who showed him Lupu's mother's picture. There was much gesturing, posturing, and hand waving before Enzo returned.

"He does not know where your cousin lives," Enzo said.

"So, he's never seen her?" Stephan said.

"Oh, he has seen her many times. He just does not know where she lives."

Kat slammed her fist into her hand. "Damn. Let me check the other numbers on the tattoo." She took out her phone and looked at Enzo. "Can you find an address with three five one eight?"

Enzo checked his Google map. "No, I have nothing, not even close."

Stephan guided Kat out of the shop and into the street. "I think maybe we need that coffee now. How about we try all the numbers in the tattoo in random order and see what we can find?"

"*Scheiße*! That bitch Hanna is screwing with us. I thought this would be easy. Why would she set a trap and make it difficult for me to find her?" Kat said.

"You think this is about you?" Stephan asked.

"Of course it is. You were there when we killed her parents. It was an accident, but she blames us."

"I thought you said she hated her parents."

Kat nodded her head. "Yes, but she hates everyone. Hanna Winter is a psychopath—she loves only herself. But she revels in the pain she gives to others."

The three stood in the street as the locals of Venice

walked around them. Seagulls floated overhead and cried into the awkward silence.

"Shall we go for that coffee now?" Enzo asked.

Kat pulled out her phone and muttered a yes as she typed a text to Bernadette Callahan.

Chapter Forty-Nine

Bernadette took Kaitlin Godwin to the hotel to put her into witness protection with Sanjay. They had to put her on the same floor as the RCMP were short staffed. She hoped neither Sanjay nor Kaitlin would make a fuss about being close together.

Bernadette made a of point of asking the officer on duty not to inform either of them.

She was about to leave the hotel when she got the text from Kat. Bernadette sighed, turned around, and knocked on Sanjay's door.

He opened the door with a grin. "I heard from Bryson. He is okay. I'm so happy you found him."

Bernadette walked into the room. "Bryson will be at the Victoria Hospital for a few days under observation. He has a broken rib and a sprained wrist."

"And that snake of a female, Kaitlin? What of her?" Sanjay asked.

Bernadette shook her head and pointed behind her.

"She is in the room across the hall. We need to keep her safe until we find some closure on this case."

Sanjay's eyes went wide. "You brought her here. Do you know the forces of evil that Hanna Winter will bring down to destroy anyone near her? Look what happened to Bryson. Why do you not see the signs? I am an accountant, and I know you are on the wrong side of the balance sheet in a shit show!"

Bernadette clasped her hands together and waited for him to finish. He ranted and raved across the room, threw a bowl of popcorn at the television, and stopped with his chest heaving.

"We need to keep you both safe. The main reason I'm here is to find out what your entry code number was to the apartment where you met Bryson."

"Why do you need that?"

"Oh, let's just call it nosey police business. Now, how about that number?" Bernadette said as her patience was wearing thin.

Sanjay shrugged. "Sure, it's one eight eight seven. I know it off by heart."

Bernadette pulled out her phone and looked at the numbers from Kat's tattoo.

"Your numbers make little sense."

"They do to me."

"No, I mean, they make little sense to the riddle we are trying to solve," Bernadette said.

"Is it something to do with the numbers other than the shipping containers?"

"Yes, but they can't seem to make the numbers match anything."

"That's because you don't understand that they used a number that was personal to me. Someone at Paradis

Transport used the last two digits of my date of birth. I was born in 1987. My code is 1987."

"How did you come upon that?"

"I look at numbers all day. Whoever made up my code knew my year of birth."

"Damn it, Kaitlin must have another code," Bernadette said. She ran across the corridor and pounded on Kaitlin's door. When her door opened, Bernadette pushed her inside and closed the door.

"You have another code—don't you?"

Kaitlin backed into her room. "Wait, what do you mean? I gave you the code."

"What year were you born?"

"What the hell? Why are you asking that?"

"Remember that story about people's lives in danger? They are still in danger—what year were you born?"

"I was born in 1992."

"Do you have a passcode that ends in 92?"

" Well, yeah, it's the code to get into the garage of the apartment, it's 1992."

"Who gave you the passcodes?"

"Deidre Frank. She had all the codes and changed them when needed."

"Did she ever change yours?"

Kaitlin grabbed a bottle of water and gulped. "No, she never changed my password for the apartment or the garage."

"Thanks, you've been a great help; sorry if I scared you." Bernadette put her hand on her shoulder, smiled and turned and left. She got into the elevator and texted the two codes with who they belonged to Kat Sager, hoping they might work to find the shipping containers.

Bernadette sent a text to Chris that she was back in

town, and she'd placed Kaitlin into protective custody and was heading home.

She'd only been away for twelve hours but she couldn't wait to get back home, although she worried about the chaos that her Grandmother Moses might cause in the same house as Chris's mother, Marula Christakos.

Marula, being Greek, insisted that her granddaughter, Raven, was raised as a Greek. So far, none of that was happening. Bernadette was letting Raven find her own way, and she was doing a wonderful job.

A text appeared on her phone. "Your grandmother is performing a smudging ceremony; I hope you can be home soon."

Bernadette ran out of the elevator and jumped into her car. "Oh crap, it's worse than I thought."

Chapter Fifty

Bernadette pulled into the yard of the acreage, parked the Jeep, and hurried to the house. The smell of sweet grass, sage, and tobacco wafted in the air as she opened the door. Grandmother Moses, in her usual attire of print dress, sneakers and hair in a braid, was waving a bowl of smoke over Chris with one hand and spreading the contrails of herbs into the air with an eagle feather.

Marula Christakos stood by the door of the library with a look of fear on her face. "What is this? How can this be helpful to have these smells in the house? We have a child in here."

Bernadette patted her shoulder to calm her down. "It's okay, Marula, this is a native tradition to cleanse negative energy. My grandmother wants to make sure Chris's wound will heal."

Marula backed away from the door. "I am making Chris my avgolemono Greek lemon chicken soup. This will cleanse away more negative energy than any tobacco smoke."

Bernadette watched Marula enter the kitchen, and she turned to her grandmother. "Grandma, I know you're trying to cleanse the negative energy of Chris's mother. You need to give her a chance."

Grandmother Moses wafted the smoke around the room and spoke as if in a trance. "I gave her lots of chances. She has been putting bad medicine into your home with insulting and discouraging words. I am making her words and negative energy disappear."

Bernadette looked at Chris. "Did you hear anything from Marula that set my grandma off?"

"My mother went off on a tangent when she found out we hadn't baptized Raven," Chris said with a sigh.

"Oops, that is something we forgot to tell her. We knew it would come up. Remember, we thought we'd let Raven decide what spiritual path she wanted to follow."

Chris adjusted his leg on the pillow and took her hand. "We will be fine. My mother will get over the news, and we will go back to our lives of quiet desperation, raising a heathen child."

"Oh, you are so funny," Bernadette said as she kissed him and ran her hand over his forehead. "How are you feeling?"

"Feeling good, but the nurse informed me this morning about my convalescence jail time."

"Great way to frame it, I guess, what is your sentence?"

"She told me three to four weeks. I can move around tomorrow, but I can only do some short walks around the house until next week."

"That doesn't sound too bad. I think I can handle you for four weeks," Bernadette said with a smile.

"Ah, no, you can't. I mean, I know you're able," Chris added with hesitation in his voice.

Bernadette put her hands on her hips. "Just what are you getting at, big guy?"

"You've only been back to work for a few days. If you take a month off to look after me, it will be without pay. You went back to work because of the bills from the new roof and vet bills for the horses."

Bernadette nodded her head and pursed her lips. "Yes, keeping a dry roof over our heads and looking after three horses comes at a price. But I want to look after you. How will you cope with the dueling grandmas?"

Chris winked at Bernadette. "Because I know my mother's tipping point for confrontation. Your Grandmother Moses has already pushed her close to the edge with the smudging ceremony. And tomorrow, your grandmother promised Raven, she would show her how to make pemmican and jerky with the moose meat the constable gave us."

"Oh my God, the house is going to reek of moose," Bernadette said.

"I'm sure my mother will book a plane ticket out of here. I told Harvey to make himself available to take her to the airport."

Bernadette chuckled. "You're probably right. But that still leaves you with my grandmother."

"We get along fine. She only speaks to me when she needs to, and the rest of the time, she plays with Raven, who adores her. I will get four weeks of fabulous rest as I convalesce, read books, and get stronger."

"You have this all figured out. I'm supposed to return to work, pretending everything is fine here."

Chris put his hand on Bernadette's arm. "Look. I know everything isn't working on your case right now."

"How do you know that?"

"I always know the minute you walk in the door how your cases are coming along. I can see from those frown lines that something is bugging you. Get back to work and solve your puzzle."

Bernadette chuckled. "You are right. Someone at Paradis Transport holds the key to a puzzle. Tomorrow, I'm going to do some digging."

Bernadette went to their upstairs bedroom, pulled out her laptop and punched in the name Diedre Frank. Nothing came up. No Facebook, Instagram or any other social media site triggered her name.

Chapter Fifty-One

A cloud of steam rose into the air from the espresso machine, filling the cafe with the heady aroma of morning coffee. Kat Sager sipped her cappuccino and wiped a bit of foam off her upper lip. The Italian cornetto was as delicious as Enzo had promised. Sweeter with a hint of vanilla and a divine marriage with the strong coffee.

Katriona Sager, the hard-driving detective from Berlin, briefly traveled back to a time when her parents were happily married, and they had savored this miracle of caffeine and sugar.

Stephan broke her trance with a question. "Did you find any new numbers we can use?"

Kat pulled out her phone and checked her texts. "Yes, Detective Callahan sent me a number from Kaitlin Godwin. Her code was one eight nine two."

"Where does she fit among your suspects?" Enzo asked.

"She was the lover of Armand Paradis, and Hanna Winter doesn't like competition," Kat said.

"Ah, her number will be *in molto important!*" Enzo said

with an Italian flourish of his hand that scattered cornetto crumbs across the table.

"Why would her number be the most important?" Stephan asked.

"From what you have told me about the woman, Hanna Winter, she must hate this Kaitlin woman the most. In Italy, a woman's scorn is fierce."

Kat turned to Enzo. "I think you have something. Are there any addresses that match her code?"

Enzo entered the number into his Google map. "Nothing."

"What if it's a number we used to find the address? What if we divided her number by something?" Stephan asked.

"I felt the number we use will have something to do with the murder of the person who started all this," Kat said.

"What do we know about that murder?" Stephan asked.

"Not enough. I need more details," Kat said as she tapped the number of Bernadette Callahan into her phone.

The phone rang four times before a sleepy Bernadette answered. "Why did I know you'd call me at this hour?"

"You could have put your phone on do not disturb," Kat answered.

Bernadette rubbed her eyes. "I knew you'd call. What do you need?"

"We need details of the murder that started your investigation. Can you give me any numbers associated with it, perhaps the age of the victim, the time of day or anything else we could use?"

Bernadette swung her feet over the bed, turned on her light and pulled her notes from her side table. She was glad Chris was sleeping downstairs. "Okay, Eric was twenty-eight years old. The murder was on July 17th, two years ago. He lived in apartment 1023 on the tenth floor. He fell ten floors to his death—do you need anything else?"

"I think that is enough for now. Thank you."

"Great, I'll see if I can get back to sleep."

Kat looked up from her phone. "Did you hear the numbers?"

"Yes, I have them," Stephan replied. He pulled out a pen and paper. "We need to get busy.

"I will order more coffee," Enzo offered.

The next two hours went by at a snail's pace. Kat and Stephan threw numbers out as Enzo checked his Google App. They were getting nowhere as the lunchtime crowd filtered in. Kat ordered sandwiches and wine to keep the cafe owner happy.

"What are we missing?" Stephan asked.

Kat pushed away her empty plate and rubbed her eyes. "We keep trying to divide one number by the next and turn them inside out. Still, they make no sense, and we are getting nowhere." She looked at her watch. "It's already past noon. We have only a few more hours until Hanna pulls the plug on innocent people."

"Wait!" Stephan said. "What is the number of the apartment you said this Kaitlin was meeting with Armand Paradis?"

Kat grabbed her phone and dialed Bernadette. "I need the apartment number where Kaitlin was screwing Armand."

"Well, and good morning to you," Bernadette replied. She reached over to her notes on the bedside table. "The apartment number was eleven sixteen."

"Sorry for waking you again," Kat said.

"No problem. I had a sleepless night, and it's six in the morning. Time for me to get up. Let me know how your search unfolds," Bernadette said as she clicked off her phone and headed for the bathroom.

Kat looked up. "Eleven sixteen. What can we do with that number?"

Stephan grabbed his pen and scribbled. "What if you subtracted Kaitlin's entry code from the floor number?"

"You get eight, two, six, and there's no such address that starts with that number in Venice," Enzo replied, shaking his head.

"Multiple the number by ten, that's the number of floors the victim fell.

Stephan scribbled on his pad. "I get 8260. There's no such address."

Stephen looked at his watch, "Kat, we are running out of time."

Kat looked at Stephen. "The last part of the puzzle has to deal with you and me...it's got to be something personal...wait, we shot both her parents. That's it. Enzo, divide the number by two."

"I got it," Enzo almost yelled. "Four one three zero is an apartment two streets from the mask shop."

Stephan shook his head. "I find it hard to believe this is so convoluted."

"Because Hanna Winter enjoys playing games," Kat said.

"Should we call Berlin? They could get us help from the Italian police," Stephan said.

Kat shook her head. "We don't have enough time, and my director is pissed at me. Stephan, you and I will go in alone. Enzo will call in the local police if we don't come out."

"I will go in with you," Enzo said.

"No, Enzo, we can't involve you in this," Kat said as she placed her hand on his. "We brought you in as our guide. Now, we must confront Hanna Winter and any of her gang she has surrounded herself with. This will be dangerous."

Enzo bristled at her words. "I was a member of the Italian Special Forces, the *Teseo Tesei*, for many years. I have never shirked my duty, and I will not let you enter danger without my help at your back."

Kat nodded her head. "*Andiamo!*"

Chapter Fifty-Two

Enzo led the way as they ran across the Rialto Bridge back into the district of San Polo. Tourists gave them a strange look and shook their heads as they raced by. In Venice, people stroll, savor, and photograph the city — they consider running a sacrilege.

Twenty minutes later, they came to a narrow alley, where there were no shops or cafes and little foot traffic. Kat noted this was the perfect place for Lupu to have hidden his mother, and it would be much cheaper than an apartment with a canal view.

"We have ninety minutes before Hanna Winter claims the container will shut down its air supply. Enzo, can you see where the apartment is?"

"The last one, at the end of the alley," Enzo said with a motion of his eyes.

Stephan and Kat followed Enzo to a dark building with shuttered windows. One entrance with double doors showed numbers of apartments on the door frame.

Enzo checked the numbers. "Yes, it is on the fourth

floor." He pulled out his handgun, checked the chamber, and pushed the door open.

Kat chambered a round in her Glock, and Stephan did the same. They followed Enzo into a dark hallway to a narrow staircase. Enzo poked his head around the stair rail and announced it clear.

They advanced in single file up the stairs, with Enzo leading the way. Kat found his transformation amazing. He'd started this morning as their chauffeur and guide, and now he'd morphed into his former self as Italian Special Forces.

They reached the second floor. A door opened. An elderly woman stepped into the hallway. Enzo hid his gun behind his back, signaling them to follow his lead. He greeted the woman with a smile and a *buon giorno* and moved up the stairway.

Returning the smile, the woman descended the stairs. They waited until she'd left the building and continued their ascent. Enzo put his hands to his lips for silence as they crept up the door of 4130. He placed his ear to the door and whispered, "I hear nothing."

Kat signaled for him to move away from the door she intended to kick in. Enzo stopped her. He tried the doorknob; it was open.

Enzo pushed the door open. The apartment was dark. He motioned for them to follow him. They formed a line of attack and advanced.

A narrow hallway opened into a living room. Kat could see something or someone in a chair facing a shuttered window. She breathed in slowly and tried to relax her finger on her gun. Her skin tingled.

Ancient floorboards creaked as they crept forward. Every moan of the floor sounded like a gunshot. Kat sensed danger. Two doors lined the hallway. She tapped Enzo on the shoulder and hand signaled that he should open the first door before going further.

Enzo placed his hand on the door and exerted force. The lights went out.

A weighted net fell from the ceiling, trapping them underneath. Two men with night vision goggles stripped their guns and knocked them out.

Chapter Fifty-Three

Kat woke up tied to a chair with Stephan and Enzo on either side of her. An old woman who looked like Lupu's mother sat in a chair across the room with a scowl of hatred. The space was enormous. A single pedestal occupied the middle of the room with a laptop computer.

Hanna Winter walked into the room with two men holding guns at her side. "Well, how fortunate to meet Katriona Sager, who was part of the dreaded Berlin B.K.A."

She pulled up a chair, turned it around and straddled it. Hanna was dressed in leather jacket, pants and boots that gave her a menacing look. "I knew you wouldn't bust in here with a large force. You are a lone wolf like me, you savored the thrill of capturing or killing me on your own. But now, I get the satisfaction of ending your life," She produced a long commando knife and balanced it in her hand. "I have fantasized how I would kill you."

Silence fell over the room as Hanna looked from one

victim to the other. She put the blade to her lips, kissed the dark metal and smiled.

"Who wants to be first?" Hanna asked.

"Are you good with that knife?" Kat asked.

Hanna laughed. "Why? Do you want to see me kill your friends before I get to you? One swipe of this knife across their jugular will be sufficient for a slow death. Do you imagine the sound of the air escaping from their lungs, is that what you long to hear?"

Kat locked eyes with Hanna and shrugged. "I wondered if you want to take me on in a knife fight."

"Ha, I love it. The incredible Katriona Sager challenges me to a duel to the death with a combat knife. No, I don't like my chances. The police academy trained you well. I would not survive such a fight."

"Then what about those swords on the wall? I read your bio; you led your university in swordsmanship, and you almost made the German Olympic team," Kat said.

"Ah, now that would be interesting," Hanna said. Her gaze shifted to the two sabers adorning the room's wall. She walked to the wall and removed the swords. "How interesting. These sabers were not designed for fencing. They are extremely sharp."

Hanna checked the blade and did a series of quick sword maneuvers. She looked masterful and at ease.

Stephan leaned over to Kat. "Have you ever fenced with sabers?"

"No, I've been involved in Kendo for years."

"But Kendo is the Japanese practice of fighting with a bamboo pole. That is a sharp sword that will cut through you, not give you a welt," Stephan said.

Kat turned to Stephan. "Kendo may be the practice of

fighting, but I have some tricks up my sleeve. If I don't try, we are dead anyway."

"May the odds be in your favor," Stephan said with a nod.

"Cut her loose," Hanna yelled at her two men.

"I want your word that if I win, you will let all of us go. That includes Lupu's mother in the corner. And I want access to the laptop to stop the countdown on the containers."

"You ask for an awful lot for a woman who is about to die. But yes, if you disarm me or kill me, no harm will come to you or Lupu's mother, but she will try to kill you because she thinks you murdered her son. And the laptop is yours to save the people trapped in the shipping containers in Hamburg. My man, Cezar, has the codes, and Bogdan will see he gives them to you," Hanna said, motioning to the two men behind her.

Kat looked at the men. She recognized Bodgan Dalca, with his bald head and serpent tattoo on his neck. He was the one in the video who had tried to enter her apartment in Berlin and murdered the night security guard.

Revulsion and anger flooded over Kat. The security guard was an elderly man named Herman Handshuh with an ailing wife, a daughter and three grandchildren. Bodgan had executed Herman in cold blood. There was a special place in hell for him, and Kat would love to put him there.

Cezar freed Kat from her bonds. She rubbed her hands and shook them to return their blood flow. Hanna walked into the center of the room.

Hanna swiped her sword through the air, dropped into a fencer's pose and smiled. "En Gärde!"

Chapter Fifty-Four

Kat examined her sword. "I see this is not a true fencing sword. It is a Kriegsmesser or War Knife made from cold steel with a Nagel or nail instead of a proper bell guard."

Hanna remained in her crouched position, ready to leap forward. Her eyes twitched at the sounds of Kat's voice. Every fiber of Hanna was ready to do battle—not talk.

Kat ran her hand over the blade. "I can't imagine a sword of this caliber was a gift by Lupu to his mother."

Hanna stood and lowered her sword. "Okay, okay. I planted them in your line of vision so I could kill you with them. Does that make you feel better?"

"Yes, it does, and it fits your personality trait of the alpha female trying to exert control over every situation. Is that why you provided the tattoo on my buttocks and the mystery of trying to solve the secret to this address?"

Hanna resumed her fencing stance. "Yes, all of what you say is true, but if you do not provide me with an adequate defense, I will run you through."

"I believe you," Kat said as she looked around the

room. "I realize now that this room was designed just for this fencing match. You must have planned this for some time."

Hanna leaped toward Kat with her sword raised. The blade flashed toward Kat's head.

Kat raised her blade. Cold steel clanged. Kat drove her elbow at Hanna's jaw as she continued her charge forward.

A crunch of bone on bone sounded through the room. Hanna fell to the floor. She jumped up with a roar of rage.

Hanna's blade flashed in the light as she attempted a swiping side slash at Kat's abdomen. Kat deflected the blade at the last second.

Silence engulfed the room. Enzo and Stephan threw furtive glances at each other. They hoped Kat could defeat Hanna but doubted the two men would keep their word.

Hanna backed into the middle of the room. "I see you are more of an adversary than I thought. Killing you will be enjoyable."

"I do not intend to die today, Hanna," Kat said with as much bravado as she could muster. She swallowed hard and focused.

Hanna stepped back, pulled out her commando knife and hurled it at Kat. The knife whooshed past Kat's right ear and planted itself in something with a thud. There was a gurgling sound.

Kat whirled to see Hanna's commando knife sticking out of Cezar's throat. The man grasped at the knife and tried to breathe with the blade lodged in his trachea.

"He is going to suffocate if you do nothing," Kat said.

"Bodgan, take care of Cezar," Hanna commanded.

Bodgan raised his Glock handgun with a silencer and shot Cezar in the head.

Hanna raised her sword. "There, he is taken care of; now, let's focus on the fight."

Kat swished her blade and circled the room around Hanna. "You are a cold bitch, Hanna. I wonder if you thought about the symmetry of this room when you set up this trap?"

"Keep talking, Katriona Sager. You are muttering your last words."

"There is little natural light. That makes these lights overhead your only source. What if they became dark?"

"You are keeping yourself from the fight with your talk. En Gärde!" Hanna yelled with her sword raised.

"I see you need a practical demonstration," Kat said. With a swipe of her sword, she smashed the bulb of the ancient light fixture above her. The center of the room was plunged in darkness; the two combatants faced each other as silhouettes.

"Bogdan, get me some light!" Hanna screamed.

"This is more interesting, don't you think, Hanna?"

Kat charged toward Hanna with her sword raised. Hanna tried to parry it; the blade cut into her arm.

"Damn you, bitch!" Hanna yelled. "Now, I will show you no mercy. I will kill you and cut the heads off your friends."

Kat didn't answer. She retreated backward to the last ceiling fixture. "To kill me, you must find me." With a flick of her sword, she smashed the last light in the room. The room plunged into darkness.

"Bogdan, turn on your cell phone light," Hanna commanded.

Bogdan fumbled with his cell phone. Stephan tipped his chair toward him, causing him to fall and lose his phone.

Kat crawled along the floor toward the noise. "Stephan, call out to me."

"I'm on the floor."

Kat crawled beside him and cut off his bonds, whirled around and did the same for Enzo. "You must overpower Bogdan before he finds some light. Hanna means to kill us all."

Hanna swished her sword in the room. "Bogdan, shoot them. They have untied themselves!"

Gunfire lit up the room. In a flash, Kat saw Bogdan with his gun. Enzo jumped him from behind and put him in a sleeper hold. There was silence.

"Stephan, Enzo, are you okay?" Kat asked.

Chapter Fifty-Five

Enzo held up a small LED light he'd found on Bogdan. He glanced at the forms in the room. Bogdan was neutralized, leaving only Hanna to be accounted for.

"Where is Hanna?" Kat asked.

Enzo swept the room with the light. Stephan opened a large, shuttered window to allow natural light into the room. The mother of Lupu sat with her head bowed forward, a pool of blood at her feet.

Stephan checked her pulse. "She's dead. Caught a bullet in the head."

Kat ran to the center of the room. "There's a blood trail. It leads to this wall." She kicked a panel, and it opened inward. "There's a tunnel here. It leads to a set of stairs."

They heard a boat's engine growl and speed away. Stephan looked out the window. "I think I see the back of Hanna Winter's head." He turned and hurried to the laptop and opened it see a countdown on the screen. "We need to focus on getting the countdown stopped."

Kat went to Stephan's side as he punched in passwords. "What about the numbers we used to find this address?"

Stephan's finger flew over the keyboard as he punched in all the number variations they had used that morning. "No, not a thing. Any other ideas?"

Kat blew out a breath. "It has to be weird and personal, something or someone she hates or loves."

Stephan looked at her. "She hates you and the detective in Canada. I'll try some of those."

He typed in their names and then started placing random numbers at the end. Nothing happened.

Stephan raised his head and rubbed the back of his neck. "I am out of ideas."

"Do you know anyone she was in love with?" Enzo asked.

Kat pulled out her phone. "I will find out." She dialed Bernadette Callahan's number.

"How is it going?" Bernadette asked.

"Winter escaped. I have the laptop and need a password. Do you remember who Hanna was in love with back in Canada? We have only a few minutes to solve this."

"Yes, his name was Matthew Paradis, the son of Armand Paradis."

"I remember that name. Was she not a suspect in his death?"

"That's how I found out about her. She left town one week before the murder of Matthew and his brother seven years ago."

Kat turned to Stephan. "Put in Matthew and subtract seven years from the current year."

"Nothing."

"How old was Matthew when he died?"

"Hold on a minute, I have to grab my file; it's upstairs."

"We have two minutes," Stephan said as he looked at his watch.

Kat nodded her head at the information and took a breath. There was nothing more they could do.

"Matthew was twenty years old," Bernadette said into the phone with a voice that sounded out of breath.

"Did you get that?" Kat asked Stephan.

"Got it!" Stephan said as he punched in the new password. "Accepted."

The laptop screen came alive with ten containers. Stephan put a stop on the computer countdown and breathed a sigh of relief. "I can't believe she would have let all of those people die just to get back at you."

"Did it work?" Bernadette asked on the other end of the phone.

"Yes, thank you. That was the password. We hope we saved all the people Hanna claimed were in containers. Our force in Hamburg will confirm once they have located them."

Bernadette sat on the edge of the bed and looked out the window as the snow fell. "What was this all about?"

"She wanted to kill me," Kat said. "It would have settled her vendetta against me. But now I have nothing. You started this case with a cold case murder, and I have a dead suspect and no leads."

"You just gave me a new lead," Bernadette said.

"The password for the computer was the name and age of Matthew. I think he meant a lot to her. Otherwise, she would have used a random password generator," Kat replied.

"That fits her personality type, but I wonder why she would use his name and age if she'd murdered him. I need to investigate this case further," Bernadette said as she wrote the information on the file.

Kat texted Director Braun in Berlin with all the locations of the containers. The BKA and Hamburg police could now set all the people in the containers free. This would be a huge coup for the Germans, and Director Braun would look like she'd saved them all. Kat couldn't care less if Braun got all the credit, lives had been saved.

Her cell phone buzzed. It was Braun.

"What happened to Hanna Winter?" Braun asked.

"Escaped. Lupu's mother and two of Hanna Winter's men died in the fight," Kat said.

Braun sighed. "Okay, I will send a team to clean up the mess. You must get out of there and return to headquarters immediately. Do you understand me?"

"*Ja, verstanden, mein Direktor,*" Kat replied in proper German with eyes rolling. Stephan stood beside her with his head shaking.

"And do not think that because you found the containers with the hostages, this case is closed. You need to clean up the mess you created. Hanna Winter is still at large. You need to find her and take her down. I expect a full report in the morning of what actions you took in Venice and what your next plan of action will be," Braun said.

"Yes, of course," Kat said and ended the call.

Stephan stood beside her. "Why did you say all of Winter's men are dead? Bogdan was fine a moment ago."

Kat turned to face him. "Bogdan is a killer. He murdered Herman Handshuh and his own man, Cezar. If the Italians or the Germans had taken him into custody, he would find a way to free himself and come after me. I have enough threats on my trail; I don't need another one."

"But you cannot shoot him; that is murder," Stephan said.

Enzo walked into the room. "No, it is what Steiner calls the brass verdict. And Katriona did not have to do it. I just shot him for all of us." He looked back to the main room, "He did call me an asshole before I shot him, but I told him at least I was not a dead asshole if that makes any difference."

"Yes, it does make a difference, to me," Stephan said. "We are police, we bring people to justice, and we do not decide what punishment they receive."

Kat shrugged and put her hand on Stephan's chest. "My dear Stephan, unfortunately, I do not agree. And this is where we part ways."

"You are not coming back to Berlin?"

"No, I plan to track down Hanna Winter. You, my lovely man, will return to Berlin. Enzo will take you to the airport and find you a commercial flight. Steiner has a private flight coming for me, and believe me, I will be staying out of Germany for a while, at least until Braun cools off."

"You were never going to keep your word to Braun, were you?"

"I only wanted to get my ass out of jail and save the people in the sea container. That is done. My life is fine without commandants and regulations, and you are welcome to join me, but I doubt you will."

"You know me too well," Stephan said.

Kat kissed him on the cheek and turned around quickly to leave.

Chapter Fifty-Six

Bernadette mused over the information that Kat Sager has sent her. The sea containers had been found, the hostages had been saved, but what caught her attention was that the codes from Kaitlin were used to find the address of the laptop and Hanna Winter.

She tucked the files under her arm and was happy to leave the mayhem of her home with the dueling grandmas and head to work that morning. She arrived in the office to see Evanston at her desk, hunched over a pile of files.

"What are you doing here? Why aren't you taking time off with Chris?" Evanston asked.

Bernadette poured herself a coffee and sat at her desk. "Chris told me to get back to work. You know the drill: bills to pay, mouths to feed, and not to mention a houseful of in-laws."

Evanston laughed. "I hear you. I wondered how soon you'd be back to work when I heard your grandmother and mother-in-law were both in town."

"What was your bet, and how much did you win?"

"Ha, I had twenty bucks on you coming in this morning. No one in the unit believed me; they took my bet at three to one. I cleaned up. Me and the hubby will dine out this weekend. Thanks for being true to form," Evanston said with a wink.

"I didn't realize I could be that predicable."

Evanston leaned forward. "In some things, not so much, but with relatives, you're an open book."

"And yet you took everyone's money?"

"Like shooting fish in a barrel. Now, what's on your mind that you raced into the unit to avoid spending quality time with your dear mother-in-law?"

Bernadette clicked the keys on her computer and brought up some files. "I don't see any interviews with Deidre Frank on either the Chan murder or the ones of Lucien and Matthew Paradis."

Evanston shrugged her shoulders. "Why would you? She works as Armand Paradis' personal secretary."

"But she played an active role in determining who would go to the apartment building where Chan was murdered. And codes she gave Sanjay and Kaitlin were used to find the sea containers. I have a feeling Frank is deeply involved in this case," Bernadette said.

"Yes, that's right, but it strikes me as kind of weird that a personal secretary to the head of the company would be looking after minor details."

"Did you notice the suit she was wearing when we served them the search warrant? Any idea what that was?" Bernadette asked.

Evanston rolled her eyes. "Damn right, I do. It was Chanel."

"How did you recognize that?"

"I saw that same jacket she was wearing in a magazine

last month; the price is the same as a tooth implant I need for my son after he took a puck in the mouth in hockey. Keep in mind that my thoughts revolve around child expenses, given that I'm a hockey mom."

Bernadette shook her head. "How much will it cost?"

"Five thousand, but our benefits cover most of it. I will stay on the force until my silly kids get older or take up playing bridge."

"Good to know. So, a personal secretary is wearing a five-thousand-dollar Chanel jacket. How much do you believe she earns?"

Evanston looked up at the ceiling as if searching for an answer. "I do not know."

"Google says it tops at eighty thousand," Bernadette said. "I looked it up this morning before I came into work."

"Doesn't sound like Chanel money."

"No, it does not," Bernadette said, placing her hands on the desk.

"Why do you suspect her?"

"She lied to me about the codes and the apartment. Claimed she had no knowledge of the place. Turns out she was sending food and wine to all those using it as their little love nest And, it's strange how the sea containers were found using access codes that only someone at Pardis Transport Company could have supplied to Hanna Winter."

"Maybe someone else in the company had access to those codes," Evanston said.

My money is on Diedre, "Did you happen to see her in that pricey Chanel jacket?" Bernadette asked with one eyebrow raised.

"You think she's more deeply involved?"

"Yeah, I do, but everything on Deidre Frank is clean. I checked her file. Her records show she's worked at the company for thirty years, is a faithful employee and has no record of anything more than a speeding ticket."

"Where did she grow up?" Evanston asked as she looked over the file.

"Kitchener, Ontario, according to her records. She came to Red Deer right out of secretarial school from Conestoga College."

"I wonder who she knew in Red Deer?" Evanston asked.

"Why?"

"Thirty years ago, this was a small town. Kitchener is just over an hour from Toronto. Deidre seems like a high-class lady. I wonder what brought her to work for Armand Paradis and his company?" Evanston said.

"Perhaps she met Armand somewhere in Eastern Canada and followed him here?"

"He's a slick character. Any idea what happened to him over in Venice?"

Bernadette drained the last of her coffee. "I never asked. He must be hiding out somewhere. We should put out a person of interest on him and maybe his lawyer will find him for us."

"What's our next move?"

"I'm going to see what Sanjay and Kaitlin have to say once they know we found the sea containers," Bernadette said as she grabbed her coat. "You want to come along?"

Evanston looked at the files on her desk. "I'd love to, but the chief wants these cleared up by lunchtime. You go have fun; do that investigation and grilling thing you love to do."

"Sure, I'll meet you back here for lunch, and you can buy with the windfall you made off your bet."

"What! Do you think I should share my winning for

betting on your neurotic behaviors?" Evanston said in mocked shame.

Bernadette headed for the door and stopped. "How about I buy lunch if you do me a favor?"

"Sure, you know I'm up for anything when you're buying lunch, as long as it isn't illegal."

"Great. Would you check the college records of Deidre Frank? I know I did a quick background check for a criminal record, and she's clean. But I'm wondering about how she got here."

Evanston shrugged. "No problem."

Bernadette continued out the door, started her Jeep and dialed Chris on her hands free.

"Hey, Bernie," Chris answered. "I wondered when you'd check in."

Bernadette sat in her Jeep as the vehicle warmed up. "I noticed it's going to turn cold this weekend. I'm wondering how we'll keep the dueling grandparents apart."

"Not a problem. Harvey is taking my mother to the airport this morning for her flight back to Toronto. I told you she would bolt if your grandma started preparing moose meat in the kitchen."

"I'm sure it was more than the moose. My grandmother can be a handful when someone gets on her bad side."

"My mother sends you her love and promises to be back when we have the christening ceremony for Raven," Chris said with a chuckle in his voice.

"Ah, so we have several years to go before…"

"She's just kidding. It's a Greek backhand comment. She'll get to a point where she must see Raven, and she will come running back here. But I'm sure mom will check to see if your grandma is here first."

"No problem, we can put out an all-clear like they do

after a tornado," Bernadette said. "I'll call you later today."
She put the Jeep in gear and headed for the hotel where
they were keeping Sanjay and Kaitlin. Everything was
pointing to an affiliation these two had with Diedre Frank,
and she needed to find out what it was.

She entered the hotel and took the elevator to the third
floor. A cleaning room cart blocked the door of Sanjay's
room. There was no RCMP officer in sight.

Bernadette hurried toward the room. A woman came
out of the room, she was dressed in a beige uniform. The
moment she saw Bernadette, she raised a gun.

Chapter Fifty-Seven

Bernadette hit the floor as a bullet lodged in the door above her head. The woman ran to the stairway. Bernadette drew her gun and started to chase but saw the body of Constable Anna Marchenko on the floor. She checked her breathing; she was fine, and there was no sign of a gunshot wound. A mark on her neck showed a taser burn.

She grabbed her radio, called for an ambulance and described the perp, then checked on Sanjay's room. He lay dead on the floor with a bullet to his head. Bernadette ran to the Kaitlin's room and pounded on the door. There was no answer.

The manager came out of the elevator as Bernadette pounded on the door. "What's happening?"

"Someone murdered one of our witnesses. I need to check on this person."

The manager fumbled in his pocket and pulled out his key card. He swiped it and backed away.

Bernadette ran into the room and swept the room with

her gun. The toilet flushed. The door opened, and Kaitlin stepped out.

"What's all the pounding about?" she asked.

"Someone murdered Sanjay," Bernadette said as she dropped her gun. "A woman dressed in a housekeeper's uniform shot him. I wanted to make sure you're safe."

She turned and walked back to the manager. "Where is the person who cleans this room?"

The manager's face turned white. "Oh my God, that's Eleanor's cart. I need to check on her."

"Where does she leave her cleaning cart?" Bernadette asked.

The manager led Bernadette to the housekeeping room. Eleanor lay unconscious on the floor in her underwear.

Bernadette walked back to Sanjay's room to see the S.W.A.T. arrive with the medics. She kneeled by Constable Marchenko as they revived her and put her on a stretcher.

"Did you see the woman who tasered you?" Bernadette asked.

Marchenko closed and opened her eyes. She couldn't move her neck. "I noticed her coming down the hall. She never looked up at me. I glanced away briefly, and she surprised me with a taser from behind."

"You're lucky she only tasered you," Bernadette said. "She fired a gun at me with a silencer."

"I heard she killed Sanjay. Sorry, I screwed up," Marchenko said as a tear fell down her cheek.

"We are understaffed, constable. You did your best," Bernadette said. Her heart sank at the constable's words. She had made a rookie mistake of taking her eye off someone as they approached, and this would not reflect well on her record.

Evanston came up the stairwell. "We didn't find the

uniform or a wig if she was wearing one, and there were no witnesses who saw her coming out of the hotel."

"Damn, I can't believe we let someone get close to Sanjay," Bernadette said. She walked into the hotel room to examine the lifeless form of Sanjay on the floor. He was lying on his back with a bullet hole in his head. "The shot was fired at close range—Sanjay must have known the shooter. He would have made a run for it otherwise."

"Who do you like for this?" Evanston asked.

"Deidre Frank. The shooter had similarities in height and weight. I was hugging the floor to avoid a bullet, but my instincts tell me we need to find her."

"I'm on it. I'll contact her office," Evanston said. She pulled out her cell phone and dialed as the crime scene investigators and the coroner entered the room.

Evanston returned to Bernadette's side. "Paradis Transport office claims Deidre Frank is taking a health day."

"Sounds like a day to end someone's health and improve her own. Let's go find her," Bernadette said.

They had a brief meeting with another sergeant to take over the crime scene, then rushed to Bernadette's vehicle and fired up the engine.

"Did her office give you an idea of what her health day entailed?" Bernadette asked.

Evanston rolled her eyes. "Magic fingers massage and nail spa."

"Let's start there," Bernadette said.

Bernadette put the Jeep in gear and spun the wheels out of the snow-covered parking lot. They hit the highway with lights flashing and weaving through traffic.

Ten minutes later, they arrived at the spa. Evanston ran into the spa. Several women looked up at her in amazement as she flashed her badge at the front desk. Tami, with green hair and lashes so long they could knock down a low-flying bird, confirmed Frank was not there.

"The front desk claims she left an hour ago for a restaurant," Evanston said when she got back in the Jeep.

"That's convenient. Did they say where?"

"Yeah, it's the little hash house we go to for a late breakfast on Main."

Bernadette left the siren off and cruised to the restaurant a few minutes later. Deidre Frank was sitting at a table near the window with a glass of wine.

"There goes our idea of her being a suspect in killing Sanjay," Evanston said.

Bernadette parked in front and opened the door. "I need a closer look; if she's legit, we move on, but I have my doubts about this convenient wellness day of hers."

Chapter Fifty-Eight

Bernadette led the way to Deidre's table, with Evanston behind her. "You mind if we join you?"

Deidre smiled at them. "Well, of course. To what do I owe the pleasure of your company? Are you taking time off from your duties?"

"No, we are chasing the murderer of Sanjay Chadha," Bernadette said as she dropped into the chair in front of Deidre and leveled her gaze at her.

"Oh my, how did it happen?"

"Someone shot Sanjay at close range in his hotel room an hour ago," Evanston said.

Deidre wiped her lips with her napkin and brushed her hand across her brow. "How awful. Who would do this? It's beyond imagination."

Bernadette shrugged her shoulders and looked at Evanston. "We were wondering the same thing. The massage place said you left an hour ago. How long have you been here?"

"You don't think I could do such a thing."

"We have a habit of asking everyone when it comes to murder," Bernadette said with a wink.

Deidre sipped her coffee, took a deep breath and pursed her lips, waiting for the detectives to get to the point and looked annoyed.

"Just tell us how long you've been here and what you did after leaving your massage," Evanston said.

"Very well, if you wish to ruin my peaceful day after my massage and nails, I will give you all the details. However, I doubt it will help poor Sanjay. I left the spa an hour ago, gassed up my car, did the drive-through at the car wash and arrived here twenty minutes ago."

"And you have receipts for all of this?" Bernadette asked.

"Of course, it's all on my phone," Deidre said as she pulled her phone out of her purse and thrust it at Bernadette.

Bernadette scrolled down the phone and found the receipts. There were time stamps on each one. There was no way Deidre could have been the shooter. "Okay, thank you for your time."

They got back in the car and listened to the police radio broadcasting the manhunt for the killer of Sanjay Chadha. Bernadette put her hands over her eyes and sighed.

"The woman who shot at me looks like that woman in there. I was staring at a Deidre look-alike in a hotel house-keeping uniform," Bernadette said in frustration.

"Look, there are lots of doppelgangers out there, mirror images of other people. I'm supposed to have one in Cleveland, according to my aunt Martha," Evanston said.

Bernadette looked at Evanston. "Cleveland? Really?"

Evanston shrugged. "Yeah, who knows where your DNA double could be?"

"Okay, let's roll back the tape, so to speak. I see a perp just over an hour ago come out of a hotel room. She takes a shot at me, and in a flash, my mind sees the woman we just spoke to."

"There you go. Maybe Deidre has a twin. I didn't get a chance to go over her files like you asked. We need to get back to the office and check them out," Evanston said.

"I need to talk with Kaitlin Godwin and the officer who was tasered. Nothing is adding up," Bernadette said.

"Well, I get that things are odd. But if it helps, I noticed our doppelgänger in the diner swished a set of nails across her face that had a chip on the index finger," Evanston said.

"I didn't see that, but I did see sweat on her lip. I thought a massage and a mani-pedi were supposed to put you in a euphoric state," Bernadette said.

Evanston shook her head. "I couldn't tell you; the last time I had a pedicure done, the poor girl needed to almost take an electric sander to my feet. I can't say the experience was soothing. And I've had two massages in my life. They both tickled me so bad I have trauma about going back."

Bernadette put the Jeep in drive and moved into traffic. "You have a lot of issues, Evanston. Maybe you should see a shrink."

"Who has time? If I ask my husband what is wrong with me, he tells me I should get a different occupation other than a homicide detective."

"Okay, where to first, the crime scene and Kaitlin or our injured constable?"

"Let's check on the constable. We can swing by Tim Hortons for coffee and a couple of bagels. I'm dying of hunger," Evanston said.

"Got it. Caffeine, sugar, and carbs. We need to feed the brain. This case is getting too involved to work on an empty stomach."

Chapter Fifty-Nine

They rolled up on police headquarters with their bodies vibrating from a double dose of caffeine goodness. Constable Marchenko had been released from the hospital and returned to review mugshots of suspects in the murder.

Durham pulled them into his office the moment they stepped into the building.

"We recognize this is bad," Bernadette admitted before Durham could say the words.

Durham ran his hand over his bald head and looked at the floor for answers. "The inspector will request an inquiry. All our asses are on the line. Our force let someone murder our witness and get away. The steps we took were sloppy and did not meet professional standards."

"It's what we had with our manpower, Chief," Bernadette said in a defiant tone.

Durham sighed deeply. "Yeah, it's the ongoing situation we deal with. But the inspector will need to cover his ass to the head office in Ottawa. Whatever happens, my unit won't be affected. I will take the fall. All of you will be okay, your pensions will be intact, and you will keep your jobs."

"Whoa, there a minute, chief," Bernadette said, raising her hand. "Our unit followed protocol as laid out in our budget. If anyone takes heat for this, it's going to be some dumb ass politician who keeps cutting our operations cost."

Durham smiled. "Gracious speech, detective, but major screw-ups call for someone to be chopped, and I don't mind if it's me. Remember, our force gives everyone leave of absence with pay while they take years to bring a case against us. I could be at home, reading novels and working out in the gym. I'd probably live another ten years without all this grief."

"You'd die of boredom long before that happens, and you know it," Bernadette said. "Now, let me get to Constable Marchenko and start to work on solving this murder case."

Evanston and Bernadette walked out of Durham's office to find Marchenko in a small interview room. She was looking over books of mugshots.

Bernadette entered the room ahead of Evanston. "Hey, Marchenko, how are you feeling?"

Marchenko put her hand to her neck and rubbed it. "I'm fine, but those damn tasers hurt like hell. I forgot what it was like getting tasered in basic training."

"You never forget that," Bernadette said. "We have a few questions. You okay with that?"

"Sure, fire away. That was a total screwup on my part. I'd love to help solve the murder."

"You said you saw the lady from housekeeping pushing her cart toward you and looked away."

"Yeah, sorry, that wasn't in my training. We are supposed to be eyes front with anyone who approaches."

"Did something distract you?"

"Yeah, I heard a noise down the hall. Like someone was walking. I saw no one; then I was on the ground."

Bernadette turned to Evanston. "We need to get to the hotel right now—there's something I need to check."

Chapter Sixty

Heavy snow was falling, and the wind had picked up as they returned to their Jeep. Bernadette put the heater on high and hit the windshield wipers. They joined the slow-moving traffic as car and truck tires spun on the new snow.

"What do you think made the sounds that got Marchenko's attention?" Evanston asked as she peered through the windshield.

"I'm not sure, but it wasn't a ghost."

"Why is that?"

"It's a new hotel. No one has died there—until today," Bernadette said as she navigated the Jeep around a bus spinning its tires up a hill.

"Oh, I forgot, you're an expert on ghosts with the famous one you found at home. How is she doing? Wasn't her name Elsie?"

Bernadette nodded. "Yes, and I discovered she'd been murdered and dumped in a well over eighty years ago. And to answer your question, I haven't heard from her much. I think Raven makes too much racket, even for a ghost."

"That's the truth. My two boys can raise one hell of a noise. I need to step outside to hear myself think."

They entered the hotel parking lot and proceeded to the crime scene. An officer stood guard at the elevator to make sure no one entered the area, and one stood outside the hotel room where Sanjay's body had been. The coroner had moved the body to the morgue to start the autopsy.

"When can we move Kaitlin?" Evanston asked. "I'm sure she's going to be pretty anxious with Sanjay being murdered across the hall from her."

"Yeah, the unit is working on it. We have even less manpower now. But I'm sure it will be soon."

After arriving at the crime scene, Bernadette said hello to the sergeant and knocked on Kaitlin's door. She opened the door and motioned for them to come inside. A female officer was with her inside the room for added protection and her peace of mind.

"Hey, Kaitlin, how are you holding up?" Bernadette asked, putting a hand on her arm.

Kaitlin shook her head and broke into tears. "I wish I had gone far from here. I brought this to Sanjay. As soon as I came back here, Hanna Winter sent her goons to kill us both."

"Yeah, it appears so. We need to ask you a few questions," Bernadette said as she sat on a chair across from Kaitlin. She sensed a soft approach was needed. To get what she wanted, there would be roundabout questions, and she knew where to start.

Kaitlin wiped her eyes, blew her nose with a Kleenex and nodded. "Sure, what's up?"

"We never discussed how close you were to Diedre Frank."

"That's easy. We hardly knew each other," Kaitlin said as she blew her nose.

"And yet Diedre gave you access to your little love nest apartment with Armand and kept your secret for all these years. You must have had some kind of association with her."

"Well, yes, but it was regarding the apartment."

"Sanjay seemed to think you set up Chan, and he said you blackmailed him into giving you Bryson to act as your cover for your pregnancy," Bernadette said. She watched Kaitlin's reaction.

"That's insane. Sanjay was the one who offered Bryson to live with me. It was his idea all along. If he told you anything different, he's a liar."

" You mean...he was a liar," Bernadette said softly.

Kaitlin put her head in her hands and sobbed. "Oh God, yes, I mean, he was a liar. But he was probably mad at me for something."

"Because he had to give you his boyfriend to act as your fiancé to hide your affair with Armand? Would that be it?"

" Yes, I guess so..." Kaitlin said as she studied her hand.

Bernadette took a moment to let the last question settle. She had a clincher that needed setting up. She cleared her throat and waited for Kaitlin to raise her eyes to meet hers.

"So, if I circle back to a conversation I had with Deidre, she stated that she also gave Sanjay and Bryson access to the same apartment. Did you know that?"

Kaitlin wrung her hands and looked up at the ceiling. "Yes, I knew that. Bryson told me."

"Okay, so you were aware Sanjay and Bryson used the same apartment you met Armand at, and yet your paths never crossed? Is that correct?"

"I never saw them at the apartment."

"Did you know that Eric lived in the same building and one floor below you?"

"I, well, yes, I found out after he committed suicide."

"The term we are using is murder."

Kaitlin looked away. "Oh. Yes, after someone murdered him."

"So, here's what I'm trying to clear up. Sanjay told us he saw you with a package with Chan's name on it the night of his murder. Did he see you with it at the office or the apartment?"

"I do not know what you're talking about?"

"Let me repeat the question. Sanjay claimed you had a package for Chan. He implied you were to deliver it to his apartment. Do you remember this now?"

"Oh, okay, yes, now I remember. Deidre gave me a package for Chan. It was personal stuff he'd left in his office. She wanted him to have it," Kaitlin said as her face flushed a bright red.

"Thanks, we are getting somewhere. And did you deliver the package to Chan?"

"I guess I did. Yes, I dropped it off at the front desk of the apartment for him."

"The apartment has no front desk or concierge, only a mailbox and the manager's office. Who did you give the package to?"

Kaitlin stared at Bernadette. "I don't remember."

"I think you do. You dropped it off to Chan to make sure he was home. Was it Deidre who asked you to deliver the package?"

"I can't remember."

"No, you remember. But you're hiding the facts behind Chan's murder. You brought the package to his place to see if he was home. Someone was likely with you. Who was it? Was it Armand Paradis?"

"No, it wasn't Armand. He wasn't involved…" Kaitlin blurted and put her hand to her mouth.

"Okay, we are getting somewhere. Who was present at Chan's murder?"

"I'm not saying anything further until I've met with a lawyer," Kaitlin said.

"Fair enough. Let's focus on the present. You were alone in this hotel room; Sanjay was across the room, and someone murdered him."

"Ah, yes, I know that."

"Good, now, did you leave your room just before someone shot Sanjay?"

"No, I was here the whole time. I opened the door when you knocked. I was in the bathroom."

"And if I asked Corporal Marchenko if you'd left your room, what would she tell me?" Bernadette asked.

Kaitlin pursed her lips. "Oh, I forgot that I asked her if I could get a soft drink from the vending machine just down the hall—I was only out of the room for a few minutes."

"Please give the officer your cell phone. I suspect you of being an accessory to the murder of Sanjay Chadha. I'm going to check on something—I'll be right back," Bernadette said.

Chapter Sixty-One

Bernadette motioned for Evanston to follow her as she walked down the hallway toward the vending machine.

"You find something?" Evanston asked.

"I have a hunch and hope I'm right," Bernadette said as she walked with quick steps to the vending machine and took out a pair of rubber gloves.

"What is it? You need another caffeine fix?"

"No, I'm looking for a mini speaker attached to the vending machine."

"And why would you expect to find that?" Evanston asked, staring at Bernadette as if she'd lost her mind.

"Because Corporal Marchenko said she heard a sound coming down the hall that distracted her from the woman with the cleaning cart. There are no other rooms down there, only this vending machine."

"Okay, I'll help you look," Evanston said as she got on her knees to check underneath the first vending machine.

"I got it," Bernadette said as she held up a small blue cylinder and showed it to Evanston and then dropped it into an evidence bag. "This is a Bluetooth mini speaker, capable of being operated from any cell phone within ten meters. That's the distance from the cleaning lady's cart to the vending machine."

"Who do you think…" Evanston started to say and looked back at Kaitlin's room. "Ah…I see where you are going with this."

"Yes, our sweet and innocent Kaitlin asked Corporal Marchenko if she could get a soda just before our murderer came to Sanjay's room."

"So, you think Kaitlin had Sanjay killed?"

"Not even close. I think she is an accessory, and that Deidre Frank put her up to placing the speaker for the diversion. Deidre Frank is our shooter."

Evanston shook her head. "But she's got a sound alibi with the massage and at the carwash."

"An alleged alibi. We need to get descriptions of the person who was at Magic Fingers massage and to get a video from the gas station. I have a feeling we'll find another doppelgänger, and I know how it'll go."

"I'll take care of it. I look forward to outing that smug bitch, Deidre Frank," Evanston said.

"Good, I'm going back to interview Kaitlin again. She is more deeply involved in this case than I initially thought."

Chapter Sixty-Two

Bernadette entered Kaitlin's hotel room with the mini speaker in the bag and sat across from her. "I found this behind the soda machine, and I bet we'll find your prints on this. A sound from this little machine distracted our corporal, who was guarding Sanjay. That gives you an accessory to murder."

"Deidre forced me to do it," Kaitlin said.

Bernadette turned on her cell phone recorder. "I'm listening."

"She was the mastermind behind Chan's death—she threatened to kill me if I didn't help her."

Bernadette sat back in her chair. "Hm, I'm wondering who is lying to me in this case, and wait, I just realized that all of you were. Sanjay has the only alibi because he's dead. So, I'll strike him off the list."

"Seriously, I didn't think she was coming here to kill him. I thought she wanted to see him for some other reason."

"Please, you don't believe what you're saying. Let's start over. When did you plan to murder Chan?"

Kaitlin stood up and waved her arms. "Okay—okay, I'll give you everything, but I want full immunity and witness protection. There's no deal until I get that."

"If you murdered anyone, I doubt I can get you a deal," Bernadette said.

"I haven't murdered anyone. But what I'm about to give you will blow your mind. You think you're after human traffickers. You don't have a clue how big this is. There're tons of heroin being moved under your noses, and your police forces are in on it. Are you ready for that?"

"Girl, I think I can get you a deal." She walked out of the room into the hall, and called her chief and the Crown Attorney. In minutes, she had authorization for immunity.

Bernadette walked back into the room with three cokes and a bucket of ice. "You have a deal. We will take your testimony and, based on that, we will free you from prosecution and place you and your child into witness protection."

"Okay, first, let me give you the broad strokes. Human trafficking is a cover for the Paradis Transport drug trafficking. They have been running contraband for years. I learned from Dierdre that Armand started moving illegal cigarettes from the USA to Canada and then across the border from province to province. He changed into the big time when Hanna Winter arrived."

"How did Deidre become involved in all this?"

"Because Deidre has been one of the masterminds. She is not really Deidre Frank. She is Hanna Winter's aunt, Gisela München, from Berlin. Hanna Winter came here at her request."

Bernadette chuckled. "Now I realize why she claimed

she was from Kitchener in Ontario, which used to be called Berlin before the war."

"I'm glad drug traffickers have a sense of humor. Hanna came up with the idea to smuggle humans with cargo and put them into slavery or prostitution. She added heroin to the floors of the sea containers."

"So, every shipment that is caught with humans being smuggled—"

"No one considers searching for drugs. They book the sea containers into evidence and move them to a storage yard where they remove the drugs. Each container has a max load capacity of sixty thousand pounds. The floors are false with ten thousand pounds of heroin; that's a street value of eighty million dollars for one container."

"That's incredible. This makes me wonder if the race to save the people in the sea containers was real or false?"

"Oh, it was real. Hanna Winter loves the drama of someone's life in the balance. But in the end, she was moving hundreds of containers full of drugs. The ones the Germans found will end up in a storage yard, and the drugs will be gone in a week. You did Hanna Winter a favor by getting the containers full of drugs through the customs officers in the dockyard. If you hadn't cracked the code, she would probably have let the hostages die and alert the police herself to move her containers. She has all the angles.

"Damn, I need to call Germany. We'll circle back to Chan's murder in a moment," Bernadette said as she left the room.

She moved to a quiet part of the hallway to avoid the conversations of the criminal investigators and the photographer.

The third ring woke up a sleepy Kat Sager. "What the hell time is it?"

"Really early for you. Are you back in Berlin?"

"No, I am in Morrocco," Kat said as she sat up in bed and rubbed her eyes to focus. "What do you need?"

"My main suspect told me that the Sea Containers you seized in Frankfurt have tons of heroin under the floors. She claims that someone will pick up the containers from storage and transport them to the drug dealers."

"The clever bastards. I will inform the German police; this will make both our countries happy to catch both human and drug smugglers."

"Excellent, enjoy your morning. I have a murder to solve," Bernadette said as she ended the call and wondered why the German Detective was in Morocco, but she didn't have time to ask.

Chapter Sixty-Three

RCMP Detachment headquarters moved Kaitlin Godwin later that day. Bernadette booked her for accessory to murder and left her in an interview room. She knew they had only hours to put holes in Deidre's alibi and she hoped Evanston had found the key element.

Evanston walked into the Serious Crimes room an hour later with Rose Smögen, a woman the exact height, weight, and hair color of Deidre and well known to the police for previous crimes.

"What's the story about Rose?" Bernadette asked.

Evanston smiled as she poured herself a coffee. "This was easy. I interviewed the masseuse, who claimed that Rose identified herself as Deidre Frank and used a cell phone to tap for payment. She'd never met Frank before, so she assumed it was her. What Rose failed to do was cover up the black rose on her right shoulder."

"So, when you discovered the identifier marks of the rose—"

"I had our division text me Rose's mug shot from her

last arrest. That rose on her shoulder was a dead giveaway, and when I showed it to the masseuse, she gave up Smögen," Evanston said with a laugh.

"What's her story with Deidre?"

"She claims that Frank gave her a thousand bucks and a spa day. She met her later this morning behind the diner and gave her back her phone. She couldn't give her testimony fast enough when she knew she was on the hook for accessory to murder."

"I'll start the paperwork for Deidre's arrest warrant. Maybe we can get her to give us the details on the Chan murder."

"I doubt Deidre will give anything away without some hard evidence. You better hope Kaitlin has something to give us," Evanston said as she picked up paper and pen to take the statement from Smögen.

Bernadette received an arrest warrant for Deidre Frank and headed out with two uniforms, who followed her to the same apartment complex where Chan had been murdered.

Bernadette pressed the intercom for Frank's suite, noticing that the entrance of the Valley Ridge Apartments looked freshly painted and cleaned. There was no answer.

After several more tries, Bernadette called the manager, Zoe Javernick.

Javernick came out of her office with a set of keys. "You won't find Deidre at home. I saw her in the parking garage, loading two suitcases into her car. She bolted out of here fast."

Bernadette ran back to her car and called dispatch to put out an APB on Deidre Frank and called Durham's cell phone.

"There's been no sign of her," Evanston said as she drank her coffee and pushed her half-eaten bagel aside.

"We had a hit on her car's license plate heading north toward the Edmonton International Airport, but she hasn't shown up on any passenger lists," Bernadette said.

Evanston looked up from her desk. "What if she has another passport?"

Bernadette's eyes went wide. "Kaitlin told me Deidre had a German name before she came here. Let me check my notes." She grabbed her iPad and scanned her notes. "Gisela München, that's who she gave me. I'm going to check which airline is flying to Germany tonight."

"Don't you think it would be too obvious for her to fly to Germany?" Evanston asked.

"She thinks she's got a brilliant cover as a German National," Bernadette said. "And I just found a flight to Frankfurt leaving in two hours."

"Do we have enough time to get a warrant for her?"

"I'm not going to chance it. We can try over the phone on our way."

"Are you sure she's going on that plane?"

"We'll contact the airline on the way there. I bet you lunch tomorrow that she's getting on that plane with a first-class ticket."

Evanston shook her head. "Okay, I'm with you, but the roads are crap with heavy snow, and it's a one-hour drive."

"No problem. This vehicle has snow tires with ice studs. I intend to drive faster than Santa Claus with his reindeer."

"I hate it when you make allusions to Christmas when I haven't been shopping for my kids yet."

"Great, tell me all about your plans as we head down the highway."

Chapter Sixty-Four

The Jeep plowed through the fresh snow and passed several slow-moving transport trucks. Bernadette pushed the Jeep to one hundred kilometers an hour and kept it there. The tires only swayed once on the snow as they blew past a large truck. After that, they held the road like cats' paws.

Evanston sat upright in her seat. "You don't have to rush. We'll have a half-hour leeway if we keep this speed."

"You never know if we'll have to make up time in case of an accident on the highway."

"You mean if someone is driving as fast as you and loses control?" Evanston asked with an eye on the speedometer.

"Yeah, someone driving this fast without my training and these great tires—holy crap," Bernadette yelled as she swerved to dodge a truck trailer that had swung into their lane.

She turned the wheel to the left and the Jeep entered the snow-covered freeway median. The Jeep's front bumper hit the snow, and a flurry of snow shot over the windshield.

They slowed to a crawl as the automatic four-wheel-drive bit into the snow and ground their way out of the median and back onto the highway.

Evanston looked at Bernadette and released her grip on the door grab handle. "Damn, that was good driving, Bernie. I thought we were going to flip over."

"I'd like to say I thought we wouldn't, but I'm glad I kept my cool. Now, try the airline again and see if they'll give you confirmation of München."

Evanston dialed and contacted the airport. Five minutes later, she turned to Bernadette. "Well, I owe you lunch. They confirmed she is flying to Frankfurt."

"Good, let's get Edmonton Airport Police to grab here before the plane can leave; we are cutting it close."

Evanston dialed the number and spoke with the airport police. "We got the same problem we had with Chadha. We have a warrant for Deidre Frank and not her German counterpart."

"Okay, is the same guy as last time?"

"Yeah, Corporal Bunsen. You want to talk with him?"

"Put him on speaker."

Evanston put her phone on speaker.

"Corporal Bunsen. We are in pursuit of a murder suspect, also known as München, and we want to apprehend her before she lands in Germany," Bernadette said.

"I got in a lot of trouble with your antics last time," Bunsen said.

"This was cold-blooded murder, Bunsen. She did it under an assumed name."

"Okay, damn it, I'll have another tarmac delay. Get here as soon as you can," Bunsen said.

"We got our wish; they are delaying the plane," Evanston said. "Now, let's not hit the ditch before we get to the airport."

"I hear you; I'll slow down," Bernadette said. She dropped the Jeep down to eighty kilometers an hour and tucked in behind a big rig that cleared a path for them to follow. Fifteen minutes later, they arrived at the airport.

Bernadette jumped out of the Jeep, leaving the flashers on, and headed toward departures. She flashed her badge at security and ran through the duty-free stores and the length of the many gates with Evanston behind her.

"Why am I forced to view pointless cosmetics during my twelve-hour workdays?" Evanston asked as she scanned the aisle as they ran.

Bernadette laughed. "The day they use a forty-plus-year-old policewoman as a model in their cosmetic ads is the day I'll load up on their stuff—there's our gate. They're boarding."

Corporal Bunsen was waiting for them. "Your suspect is in seat 3C."

Bernadette flashed her badge at the airline flight attendants and walked onto the plane. Deidre was sipping her champagne and flipping through her phone as she walked up to her.

Bernadette leaned over her. "Hello, Deidre Frank, I'm arresting you on suspicion of murder."

Deidre looked up and smiled. "You have the wrong person. I'm Gisela München."

"That's fine, Gisela München. I'm arresting you on suspicion of being Deidre Frank, who is a suspect in a murder investigation."

"But—"

"You and Gisela have no buts left. Rose Smögen gave

up your alibi, and Kaitlin Godwin gave us your identity. Please stand up to avoid any potential damage to your beautiful Chanel suit."

"I'll just drink the last of my champagne."

"Yes, that's a good idea. Champagne won't be on the menu where you're going."

Chapter Sixty-Five

Chief of Detectives Durham looked over Bernadette's report, put it down on his desk and let his hand run over his bald head. "Forensics turned up a set of prints on the cleaner's cart in the hotel. With Kaitlin's testimony, I'm sure we can get a murder conviction for Sanjay Chadha's death, but how about Eric Chan's?"

Bernadette read from her notes. "The chemical found in Chan's bloodstream matches traces from a bottle found in Frank's apartment. Kaitlin Godwin made a written statement claiming Frank injected Chan, and Sanjay helped her toss him over the balcony. She also handed us a burner phone that Deidre Frank used that placed her at the scene at the exact time of the murder. Deidre had told Kaitlin to get rid of the phone. But she kept it for insurance."

"What was their motive?"

"Chan knew too much. According to Kaitlin, Sanjay falsified the books to hide the sea containers. Frank was trying to keep the lid on everything to keep Hanna Winter happy. Everyone was afraid Winter would come after them if they screwed up."

Durham shook his head. "But why did Sanjay and Kaitlin attempt to implicate one another? Why wouldn't they close ranks?"

"Kaitlin claims Frank told them to keep us guessing. She convinced Kaitlin to hide her pregnancy and use Sanjay's boyfriend as a ruse. It was more to keep Winter from discovering the pregnancy than anyone else."

Durham shook his head. "Did Kaitlin know anything about the cold case of the Paradis Brothers?"

"Her eyes turned murky in that subject."

"Murky?"

"Yeah, as in I could see her brain work overtime to try to remove any thoughts she had on their murders."

"You think she knows?"

"I think she has a good idea, but if I try to press it, I'll lose her cooperation on some of the inner workings of the company to nail their drug trafficking operation."

"It's a fine line we walk to find the bigger criminals over the backdrop of the number of murders they commit. If you can conclude the Chan case to the fullest, we may receive additional information if Armand Paradis appears." Durham said.

"I've requested our Crown Prosecutor contact Interpol in Europe put out a Red Notice on Armand Paradis for his involvement in drugs and human trafficking, but we've got to find him to serve it. He seems to have vanished." Bernadette said.

There was a knock on the door, Evanston poked her head in. "Bad news. Deidre Frank was murdered by another inmate in the correctional center."

Bernadette sprang out of her chair. "What the hell happened?"

Evanston stepped inside the office and closed the door behind her. "An inmate got her from behind with a shive made from a toothbrush and nailed the carotid artery in her neck. The guards didn't see her until it was too late."

"Does Kaitlin Godwin still need witness protection?" Durham asked.

"Oh yeah," Bernadette said. "The person responsible for Frank's death will seek revenge against Kaitlin."

"You don't think it was the drug dealers?"

"No, I'm positive it was Hanna Winter," Bernadette said.

Chapter Sixty-Six

Kat Sager was getting out of bed when her cell phone rang. "Ah, Detective Callahan, I'm so glad to hear from you. I have told the German police that you are the reason for one of the largest drug busts in Germany. Of course, they are not happy that we had to arrest ten crooked cops, but that is the price you pay for the big scores."

"You are welcome. I just wanted to let you know that Hanna Winter took out my suspect, Deidre Frank. But her real name was Gisela München. Does that name sound familiar?"

"Hanna Winter's mother was named München, that was probably her sister, and Hanna's aunt."

"Yes, it seems she had her own aunt murdered in jail. The woman who killed her received ten thousand dollars into her daughter's account, who has already spent most of it on booze and drugs."

"So, she was the connection to Hanna Winter in Canada. Too bad she's dead. We won't get to discover what her role was in the organization."

"It seemed it was to keep Armand Paradis from screwing up and keep everyone in line. The serious human and drug trafficking only started when Hanna Winter arrived in Canada. The aunt had the idea, but Hanna made it happen."

"Ah, that sounds like Hanna."

"Do you have a plan after this big drug bust?" Bernadette asked.

"Well, first, I plan to get a nice new tattoo on my butt to cover these crazy bogus numbers that Hanna gave me, and then I am going after Hanna Winter."

"What tattoo are you getting?"

Kat chuckled. "Well, I've had a lot of time to think about it. I have settled on a lovely Samurai Sword. There's no protection like good Japanese steel."

"Sounds nice."

"I'll send you a picture when it's done and healed."

"Well, I didn't know we were that close, but sure send me your butt photo, and I'll send you the picture of the Raven on my stomach. Perhaps they are just symbols of protection, but to me, they mean something."

"Look, whatever it takes, you need to stay safe and watch out for yourself. Anything is possible for Hanna Winter to get even with us. She tried to kill both of us two years ago, and she tried it again with me in Venice."

"I totally understand," Bernadette said. "This time, I've taken precautions around my farm. Now, what is your next move?"

"Simple, I have left the German police, which means I'm free to do as I please, which is to find Hanna Winter and kill her," Kat said.

"Don't you mean arrest?"

"Only if she gives me that option—but I hope she doesn't."

Chapter Sixty-Seven

Christmas Eve, Blue Sky Acres, Red Deer, Canada

Franco approached the lights of the farmhouse on his hands and knees. He could hear music playing within, and the smells of roasting turkey and a hint of sage filled the air, making him both hungry and angry.

A fake wolfskin blanket was tied to his back with a wolf headpiece on his head. He crawled on all fours to mimic an animal to confuse the trail cams and laser trip wires he'd seen in the woods surrounding the farm.

He'd promised Hanna Winter he would kill Bernadette Callahan, and tonight would be the night. Franco had escaped the police and healed himself in a hideout for several weeks, and now was the time. He carried an MP5 9 mm submachine gun with a silencer. Tonight's kill would be epic in the little city. He almost smiled at the headlines this little weapon would cause.

A branch made a snapping sound in the cold. He cursed

and kept an eye out for any movement in the house. He saw none and continued on his hands and knees to the house.

Harvey Mawer was in the barn tending to the horses. Bernadette Callahan walked in with Sprocket and Pepper behind her.

Harvey shook his head as he noticed the cat riding on top of the dog. "I don't think I've ever seen a cat do that?"

Bernadette looked down at the animals. "About a week ago, Pepper started to ride on Sprocket's back when they roamed the property. Grandma Moses made this quilted saddle for Pepper to ride, so the cat's paws didn't dig into Sprocket's hide."

"Very considerate of your grandma. It appears that the animals are on patrol."

"Yeah, they do several laps of the property every evening. And we find it hard to keep them in at night."

"Animals can be strange, sometimes," Harvey said as he shook some feed into the horse's stalls.

"I came to get you for dinner, Harvey. Your sweetheart told me you needed some advance notice, so you didn't arrive at the table smelling fresh from the barn," Bernadette said as she patted his shoulder.

"She's right about that. I'll go in and wash up. I'll be there right away. I never want to be late for your husband's fine cooking."

Bernadette turned to go when she looked at Sprocket and Pepper. "What's going on with you two?"

Sprocket's tail was ridged with his tail back. The big German Shepherd emitted a low growl. Pepper stood on the dog's back. Its paws spread as its claws kneaded the quilted saddle.

"Looks like they smell a coyote or fox outside. It's best to let them go outside and flush it out, otherwise they'll be howling and barking in the house all night."

Bernadette pulled out her phone and checked her alarm app. "I see a small form crawling in the trees; you're right, it's probably a coyote." She kneeled beside Sprocket. "Okay, go out there and scare away whatever's out there, but don't kill it. It's Christmas Eve; have a little mercy on the other animals."

Sprocket fixed his gaze on the barn door. Bernadette opened the door, and the dog bolted out like a cannonball.

"Now that is one determined animal. God help the poor thing that gets in his way," Harvey said as he made his way to his Carriage house to wash up.

Franco crouched behind a bush and halted. Did he see something in the shadows? He muttered a curse to the night, the cold and Hanna Winter as he sought to hide his presence. One last charge at the house, and he would be in the kill zone. Taking the gun off safety mode, he moved the pin to the rapid-fire mode and stepped from behind the bush.

Sprocket and Pepper made no sound as they closed the distance from the barn to the bush. German Shepherds have a top speed of 48 kilometers per hour. Sprocket hit 30 KM on the snow.

Franco saw the pair too late to shoot. Sprocket closed the gap as Pepper launched off his back to land on his face. His claws wrapped around his head and into his neck. His teeth clenched his nose.

Sprocket's jaws clamped 230 pounds per square inch of canine force onto Franco's privates. Pepper's fur muffled his screams. He tried to swat the cat with his gun. His finger pulled the trigger and unleashed a full clip of 9 mm bullets into his head.

Pepper jumped off just in time.

Sprocket and Pepper surveyed their vanquished foe, looked at each other and made their way back to the house.

Chapter Sixty-Eight

Marrakesh, Morocco

January, late afternoon

Katriona Sager walked through the Jemmaa el– Fnau, the largest market of Marrakesh, searching for fresh spices for the special meal that Nadia, her mother's partner would make that evening.

Nadia was a wonderful woman, a retired belly dancer with soft features and a wonderful smile. She looked after the spacious apartment in the Medina, where they preferred to live rather than the posh neighborhood of Hiverernege, a place, in their words, 'where two old lesbians would feel welcomed.'

Katriona's mother, Ilsa, had become a famous painter of modern naked women dressed in fabulous hats. Kat still couldn't understand why anyone would pay for such things, but she could not deny her mother was talented and made an enormous amount of money every month from her art.

Vendors called out to her as she wandered the long rows of stalls, haggling over prices and filling her bag. She had a momentary glimmer that this could be her life. If she quit her quest to find Hanna Winter, there was a world of possibilities. Love, family, a new business with the money her grandfather had left her, but she knew none of this would happen.

As she bought her last item, her cell phone buzzed with a text. She read it, shook her head and smiled, then dialed a number on her cell phone.

Bernadette Callahan answered the phone. "Detective Callahan, serious crimes division."

"It's me, Kat."

"I didn't recognize your number."

"You probably never will, as I change them often. I have news for you. The Venice Police discovered the body of Armand Paradis in a warehouse where Hanna Winter escaped capture. The report said he'd been dead for over a month. His body had been stuffed into a barrel of olive oil."

"How was he murdered?"

"Bullet in the back of the head," Kat said as she watched the late sun drop down over the ancient buildings surrounding the square.

"Once you discovered the heroin shipments in the sea containers, Armand was of no use to Hanna Winter," Bernadette said.

"Yes, that is the M.O. of Hanna Winter. I'm sure she will surround herself with more useful talent and find another avenue for her crimes," Kat said as she walked toward a cab.

"I take it you will be hot on the trail of Hanna soon?" Bernadette asked.

"I'm just waiting for a contact with information. As soon as I have it, I will be on my way," Kat said as she got into a taxi.

"Well, take care and keep in touch," Bernadette said.

"Of course, I want updates on that fabulous little girl of yours and your dreamy husband," Kat said with a smile.

The taxi dropped her off at the apartment. She dropped the spices in the kitchen and went into the large bedroom Ilsa and Nadia had given her. There was a bed, dresser, desk and an area with a mat for daily workouts. Kat had a Kendo bamboo practice sword where she'd resumed her daily exercises in sword technique. Beside the bed was a Samurai sword on a small stand.

Her cell phone rang. She recognized the number and smiled. "Director Braun, I got your text regarding Armand Paradis."

"It is too bad that Winter decided to use fine Italian olive oil to hide his body. Such a waste," Braun said.

"But you didn't call to comment on bad olive oil; what do you have?"

"Our cameras picked up Hanna Winter in Finland. She arrived two hours ago at the Helsinki Airport from Paris," Braun said.

"Hm, that's interesting. She wants to be seen if she arrived on a commercial airline," Kat said as she walked to her Samurai Sword and ran her finger over the blade.

"Be careful, Katriona Sager. And if you kill her, please leave no witnesses. I saw the look on Stephan's face when he filled out the report on Bogdan Dalca, he lied for you. Another police officer might not do the same, and I won't be able to help you."

"So, you will help me with intel on this?"

"Here is my offer. You have shown how valuable your investigations are by going off the grid and being a rogue officer. None of my team could have done what you did. I will place the full research and tracking capabilities of the BKA at your disposal, but I will ask you to verify with me which criminals you wish to dispose of. Some of them are useful for further intelligence. Those that are not, do with them as you wish, but don't get caught."

Kat smiled and said softly, "Ja, mein Direktor, ich verstehe. Danke."

More by Lyle Nicholson

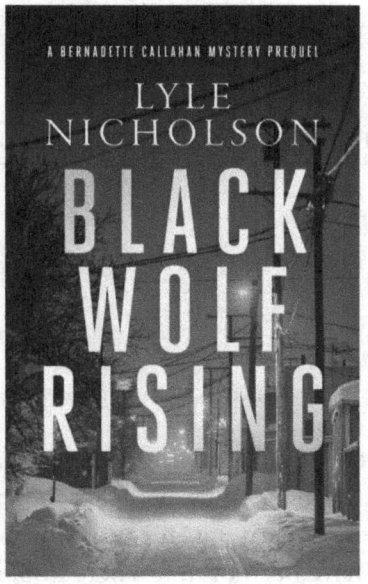

A BERNADETTE CALLAHAN MYSTERY PREQUEL

LYLE NICHOLSON

BLACK WOLF RISING

vinci-books.com/black-wolf-rising

A detective must choose between fight or flight.

As she struggles to harness the rage that has always been her downfall, Bernadette discovers the key to saving those she loves lies in confronting the very demons that haunt her past. Her greatest weapon is also her greatest vulnerability.

The gripping prequel novella to Lyle Nicholson's Bernadette Callahan series, readers are invited to witness the birth of a heroine unlike any other.

Turn the page for a free preview…

Black Wolf Rising: Chapter One

September, 1993

Bernadette's boots thudded on the hard ground. Her chest heaving, lungs burning. Why had she chosen to run? She should have stood there, taken the beating in the school-yard. It would have been over, teachers would have run out, broken it up—she would have suffered a bloody nose maybe, no problem.

But she'd kicked Tommy Cardinal in the groin. His grunt resounded around the reservation school. He'd called her father a white drunk—which was true. Then he called her mother an Indian whore.

Her foot had come up with its size-eight boot attached on its own, like a horse reacting to a slap in the hindquarters. The boot's reinforced toecap contacted Tommy's soft testicles, and he went down in a heap on the ground.

Bernadette had only seconds to stand over him grinning before Peter and Stephen Cardinal came rushing at her. They were Tommy's cousins, his guardians, and his muscle.

Tommy was the mouthpiece, a scrawny seventeen-year-old, held back several times in grade school, to be the biggest pain in the ass at Lone Pine School for First Nations children.

If she'd have stood there, Peter would have smacked her, and Stephen would have kicked her. Neither of them had the balls to beat her in the schoolyard. But she ran.

She headed down the path leading towards the river. The spruce trees swayed in the wind above her, watching her run, as if saying, "You're running into danger, turn back."

Peter and Stephen were gaining on her. They were taller, excellent runners, and both in running shoes, not boots. She dug in harder, sweat coming off her brow.

"You half-breed bitch," Peter yelled. "We're going to mess you up good this time, Bernadette."

A chill went down her spine. What would they do to her? The path to the river went downhill—she almost lost her balance, her heels dug into the hill as she descended in large leaps down the path. She could hear them breathing behind her.

She took a sharp right at the bottom of the path. There was a trapper's cabin there. Old Joe Two Feathers dried his fish there. He might be there. She'd be safe if he was.

The path narrowed. Wild rose bushes caught at her dress as she ran. Why the hell had she worn a dress? A dress with boots made her cool, but cool was stupid now. It slowed her down.

The cabin was in the distance. No smoke came from the chimney. A lump came in her throat. Joe wasn't there. She was on her own. Her boots dug into the dirt. If she could make it to the river, she could swim away from her pursuers.

She was an excellent swimmer, while Peter and Stephen could barely swim.

The path to the river was past the trapper cabin. In thirty seconds she'd be there, in a minute she'd be in the river. She never made it. She tripped over a tree root, the big boots catching it squarely and sending her falling forward into the dirt.

The fall knocked the wind out of her. She tried to get up and found four hands on her. Her run was over.

Peter turned her over like she was a rag doll. His enormous face leered down at her. "Hey, Bernadette. Got you now, bitch."

She spat at him, bared her teeth in defiance. The last thing she wanted to do was show fear. Her fists balled in readiness to strike the moment they let her go.

Peter slapped her across the face. "You dare bite me? Thought you'd got away—you're going nowhere. Now, we'll teach you a lesson, you'll never forget."

"What...what're we... gonna do to her?" Stephen asked. It seemed a matter-of-fact question. He was out of breath trying to catch Bernadette and wondered what the spoils of the chase would be.

"We'll wait for Tommy," Peter said.

Tommy came limping down the trail. Bernadette glared at him. Her green eyes flashing at him as he came into view.

"You caught the piece of shit. Good," Tommy screamed as he came closer.

Bernadette fought Peter's grip, but he held her down with both arms, pinning her harder to the ground. "I'll slap you again, bitch," Peter said.

Bernadette eyed her surroundings, looking for weapons. There were rocks by the trail and a large broken branch.

She took these in, judged their distance to her hands, and glared at Tommy.

"What're we gonna do to her, Tommy?" Stephen asked. "You want to get a long switch and give her ass a good few whacks?"

"Hell, no," Tommy said. "I think we're fixing to have an old-fashioned cock party." He smiled at Bernadette. "You know you've wanted me since you laid eyes on me. Now you got my attention. I'm all yours."

Bernadette spit a mouthful of blood from Peter's slap. "You think you're going to rape me, you got another think coming. I'll rip your dick off, you scrawny little shit."

"Damn it, Bernadette, this ain't rape, it's you giving the boys what they want in the woods. You know you've been longing for it. Who's going to believe a little half-breed bitch from a drunken white man and whorin' Indian woman?" Tommy asked in feigned surprise.

"Bastard," Bernadette screamed. She struggled against the grip of Peter and Stephen. They held her tight. "Pull up her dress and pull down her panties," Tommy yelled.

Peter changed his grip on Bernadette. He pulled on her dress. Her arm came off the ground. "Quit squirming, Bernadette," he yelled.

Tommy pulled his zipper down and realized he had a problem. Bernadette's kick to his testicles had produced a negative lift off in his erection. He put his hands down his pants, but nothing was being aroused.

"God dammit. She kicked the life out of my dick," Tommy said. "Peter, I'll hold her, and you do her, then Stephen can have at her, and my dick will be back in action."

"Sure thing," Peter said.

Tommy came to Bernadette's side. Her legs were

thrashing with those deadly boots. Her long, light-brown legs were showing up to her panties. The boys were licking their lips for the prize they were about to partake.

When Peter let Bernadette's arm go for Tommy to take over, Tommy wasn't fast enough to grab hold. Bernadette shot from his grip. She punched Stephen in the nose with her fist. He yelped and fell over.

She rolled off the path and picked up a rock and came at Peter's head with it. Peter was beside Tommy, his back to the bushes. He lifted one arm—too late. The rock hit Peter's head in a sickening crunch.

Bernadette grabbed the tree branch on the path, holding it high over her head, aiming it at Tommy. Tommy put his hands up in defense. She stomped on his leg with her boot. He screamed in agony and grabbed his leg. The branch came down hard on his head.

Stephen lay there, wild-eyed on the trail. "Don't hurt me, Bernadette...please...I was just along...you know...to have a little fun."

"You pathetic asshole," Bernadette screamed. She hit him hard with the branch on his body; he turned away, and she landed one on his skull. The crack of branch on bone told her she'd found her mark. He collapsed on the ground.

Bernadette stood over the three bodies. Were they just knocked out? Had she killed them? She couldn't care less. They wanted to rape her. If she had a knife right now, she'd have cut their dicks off and hung them around her belt like scalps, tribute to her victory.

She let out a bloodcurdling Indian war whoop, running down the trail and back towards her home. There would be consequences for this fight, there always were in the tiny village. She had no idea this would change her life forever.

Black Wolf Rising: Chapter Two

Morning arrived with a thunderstorm booming in the distance and a loud knock on the door. Bernadette's grandma Moses went to answer the door. She did it in the same manner she did everything, which meant in her own time.

Nothing pushed Grandma Moses except the seasons. She opened the door to stop whoever at the door was pounding on it.

Chief Dan Cardinal stood on the small wooden step. He looked larger than normal. This morning he was wearing his cowboy hat instead of his baseball hat. The cowboy hat meant he was on official business.

Grandma Moses waved him into the house and went to her wood stove to make tea. She always served tea the moment you walked into the house. You could ask for something else, but it would appear as tea.

Chief Dan followed Grandma Moses into the house and sat at the kitchen table. It was the only place to sit. Off the kitchen was a postage-stamp-size living area with an armchair, coffee table, and small television with antennas that searched in vain for fuzzy reception from down south. Grandma Moses was the one who sat in the armchair.

"There's been a problem," Chief Dan said, after clearing his throat a few times. He felt uneasy around Grandma Moses. The whole native village knew she could channel spirits. No one messed with her unless they wanted an ill omen to descend on them.

"What kinda problem?" Grandma Moses asked.

"Tommy, my boy, and his cousins, Stephen and Peter, they got beat up bad down by the river," the Chief said. His big body creaked forward in the little kitchen chair.

Grandma Moses poured the tea into cups and placed a cup for the chief. "Oh," is all she said.

"The boys say Bernadette was at the river," the chief said.

"Is that so?" Grandma Moses said as she shuffled over to the table and sat down. She didn't look a match for the chief, but she was. Grandma Moses was small, plump in the middle, and always dressed in the same shapeless, flowered dress. Her grey hair had been grey since Bernadette could remember. It had two styles, tightly woven pigtails, either up or down.

But it was her eyes. The soft brown eyes registered her slight surprise or interest with the smallest flicker. They could pierce into the heart of the biggest men and make them uneasy.

Bernadette stood in the bedroom's doorway she shared with her grandma. She could see the chief squirming.

The chief looked away from Grandma Moses and stared at Bernadette. Their mutual hatred for each other was apparent. Bernadette held his gaze and stared back at him.

"Tommy says you led Stephen and Peter to the river and some white boys from town jumped them. You want to tell your Grandma and me why you did it?" the chief said.

Bernadette held her hand to her mouth. She couldn't believe what she was hearing. Of course, how could those three idiots explain how they'd been beat up by a sixteen-year-old girl?

The chief stared at Bernadette, then looked back at Grandma Moses. "it involves the RCMP. They'll be out to question Bernadette. Look here, Grandma Moses, no one wants trouble here, but your Bernadette has brought it on herself—"

"Ha, bullshit," Bernadette yelled.

The chief winced. No one interrupted him. He could expel anyone who did it on the reservation or in council. Under the gaze of Grandma Moses, he was on shaky ground..

"I'll speak with her," Grandma Moses said. She got up from the table. The meeting was over. The chief knew it was time to leave. He put his hat on with determination, adjusted its brim, and then lumbered out the door. He slammed it as his last act of authority.

"Why didn't you tell me this last night?" Grandma Moses asked. It wasn't accusatory, just a question.

"I thought you'd think I was stupid for running from them. I shouldn't have run. Tommy called Mom a whore, so I kicked him in the balls then ran. They chased me into the woods, caught me, and said they were going to rape me..." Bernadette's voice broke as she explained.

Grandma Moses walked over and held Bernadette. She was much smaller than Bernadette, but her embrace was strong. "I'm glad you got the better of them." She stared up into Bernadette's eyes. "You should have cut their balls off."

"I didn't have a knife," Bernadette said.

A knock came at the door. Bernadette went to the door and opened it to find RCMP Sergeant McNeil at the door. She motioned for him to come in. Dryness came into the back of her throat. The lie the boys had told was manifesting ominously.

"Thanks for seeing me," the sergeant said.

As Bernadette closed the door, she could see the locals crowding around outside. She was already guilty. The crime was bringing in white boys to do her dirty work.

Sergeant McNeil looked like he'd dropped into the world, old and worn. His hair and mustache were grey, his eyes were a washed-out blue, and the man had a roadmap of worry on his wrinkled face. It was like the world's problems had settled on him and wouldn't let go.

McNeil sat at the table and removed his hat. He took out a notepad and pen and laid them out on the table. "I'm here to take your granddaughter's statement. There are no charges being laid; we need to find the facts."

Grandma Moses sat across from McNeil, shoved tea towards him. "You want to tell me what facts you're dealing with?"

McNeil raised an eyebrow at her question. He should have known Grandma Moses would cross-examine him. He'd been here several times before when Bernadette had gotten into trouble in town. He leafed through his notebook and read. "The Cardinal boys stated they chased Bernadette into the woods after she assaulted them. Deep in the woods, several boys from town jumped them and beat them unconscious."

"Bullshit," Bernadette said.

Grandma Moses put up her hand to silence Bernadette. "Tell me, Sergeant, do you believe this report?"

McNeil shook his head. "Not a word. All the teenage kids from town were away at a basketball game in La Crete. I checked with sick reports, and I have two scrawny twelve-year-olds in town. I don't think they were a threat."

"You know the Cardinal boys are lying. Why come here and make like you're on their side?" Bernadette said. She fixed her gaze on the constable with her arms crossed.

"Because I needed to talk to your grandma and you, Bernadette," McNeil said. He stirred his tea and looked across at Grandma Moses. "You know the village will discover the boys lie—don't you?"

Grandma Moses nodded her head.

McNeil continued, "they'll come after Bernadette harder next time. I'm sure whatever happened in the woods wasn't good—".

Bernadette unfolded her arms and stepped forward, "They tried to—"

"Stop!" Grandma Moses commanded.

"Did they assault you... sexually?" McNeil asked. His eyes dropped to the table with his question. He hated dealing with rape cases. They had no female officer in their detachment; it always fell on him to do investigations into rape. He was terrible at it. He was so uncomfortable in the interviews with women that few wanted to offer allegations.

Grandma Moses threw a threatening glance at Bernadette. She got the message. Her lips tightened so hard they went white. She held back a tear, trying to escape from her eye.

"Bernadette has no statement to make other than she saw nothing," Grandma Moses said.

"I leave this up to you." McNeil sighed and put away his notebook. He looked up at Bernadette. "No one ever takes the RCMP's advice, but if I can say one thing, it's get this girl out of here."

"But I didn't bring any white kids in to beat them up," Bernadette protested.

"Doesn't matter," McNeil said. "The town is already up in arms because they know it isn't true, and your reservation is ready to have me arrest Bernadette because they think it is true."

"Where's my justice?" Bernadette said.

"You shamed Chief Cardinal's son and his cousins," McNeil said. "It's your word against theirs, and they've got bruises to prove their case. Bernadette, you'll never be safe here."

"He's right, Bernadette," Grandma Moses said. "The Cardinal boys have many friends tougher than they are. If they can convince them you ambushed them, you're in big trouble." She turned to look at McNeil. "I'll send her away tomorrow."

Sergeant McNeil got up and headed towards the door. "I'm sorry it had to be this way, but perhaps it's for the best." He turned and looked at Bernadette. "Sometimes a fish becomes too big for its pond."

Bernadette stood and faced her Grandma. "What's he saying?"

"He's right. I'm going to make a phone call. Pack a bag."

Grab your copy...
vinci-books.com/black-wolf-rising

Afterword

I had to bring Bernadette Callahan and Katriona Sager back together after *The Suspect from Berlin*. So many readers wrote in how much they enjoyed the two detectives, one from Canada and one from Berlin working together on cold case mystery that involved international human trafficking.

And, as I couldn't leave my readers wondering if they'd ever track down Hanna Winter again, they did, but in Venice.

I admit, I did get a bit carried away with the butt tattoo, but this is me, and my sense of humor, who some might consider a bit dark and twisted but again…I could not resist once I had the idea.

Where will I go from here? I have a plan for another in the series, but first I will be doing a short series of new detective named Jaz Ryder in my hometown of Kelowna, British Columbia, Canada.

My little city, nestled in the Okanogan Mountains and surrounded by lakes, vineyards and orchards is the perfect place for murders. And I already have three planned.

Acknowledgments

I must thank my good friend, Jeff Bush, for his detailed help in Venice. Jeff loves Venice and takes students there on workshops. Jeff gave me reams of information on the inner working of the canals, the shops and especially the mask shops, of which he has a major collection.

And a special thanks to Rhonda Alderson who is my 2nd degree Black Belt Judo expert who helps me with all the fight scenes. Bernadette and Kat couldn't throw a proper punch without Rhonda's guidance.

I am also grateful to my Beta Readers and my Advance Review Copy Readers. You are the first eyes on my manuscripts, and I appreciate the time you spend to give me feedback.

About the Author

Lyle Nicholson writes crime and mystery books you will find hard to put down. His first book in the series, *Polar Bear Dawn*, takes place in the high Arctic of Alaska in the unforgiving winter.

The series is based on Detective Bernadette Callahan, who readers love for her hard-nosed style, and failure to follow the rules. As a female detective, she is a phenomenon in Canada's Royal Canadian Mounted Police. You will enjoy her style as she solves crimes that will take you on a world journey.

He lives in Kelowna, British Columbia with his wife, and spends much of his time cooking, enjoying fine wines and writing novels. Somehow, he calls this work!